Winter's Curse

Isla Wrenwood

Copyright © 2024 by Isla Wrenwood

All rights reserved.

No portion of this book may be reproduced in any form without written permission from the publisher or author, except as permitted by U.S. copyright law.

Contents

1. Chapter 1 — 1
2. Chapter 2 — 6
3. Chapter 3 — 15
4. Chapter 4 — 24
5. Chapter 5 — 31
6. Chapter 6 — 38
7. Chapter 7 — 47
8. Chapter 8 — 56
9. Chapter 9 — 66
10. Chapter 10 — 74
11. Chapter 11 — 84
12. Chapter 12 — 92
13. Chapter 13 — 98
14. Chapter 14 — 106
15. Chapter 15 — 113
16. Chapter 16 — 117
17. Chapter 17 — 124

18.	Chapter 18	130
19.	Chapter 19	138
20.	Chapter 20	147
21.	Chapter 21	156
22.	Chapter 22	164
23.	Epilogue	172

Chapter 1

It was the depth of winter, among the falling snow and pitch dark sky, a tale awaited to be told. A tale that began in the dead of the winter night when two people walked with their heavy snow boots in a forest filled with gigantic trees—old and majestic trees that had seen so much. The trees had lost their leaves, leaving their branches and trunk dried out by the frozen cold weather. The branches looked like hundreds of straggling dark arms and the twigs were like claws that intertwined and waved in the wind. The darkness of the branches became a beautiful contrast with the whiteness of the snow that stuck to them.

The two people, drowned in their winter coat adorned with wolves' fur and their wool shawls, walked as fast as they could in the thick snow.

It was a man and a woman.

The woman was carrying something against her chest. Something swaddled in a few layers of thick black wool blankets.

"We are almost there, Hanna," the man spoke while turning his head slightly to Hanna, he walked a step ahead of the woman and gingerly craned his neck to watch the path in front of him.

"I hope so, Garlan. I also hope there is no more blizzard, and we can do this task well ..."

The man, Garlan, stopped walking, turning to Hanna again with a deep conviction in his brown eyes. "We can. We have to do this as instructed by our lady. For the good of our kingdom and homeland."

Hanna blinked and nodded, trying hard to be brave.

"It is a great blessing from the gods above, don't you think, Hanna? We have been married for years, and we have wished and prayed and hoped for a child but the gods have not granted us our wish until now. Now we have this task ... this perfect task!" Garlan lifted his arms up to the sky as if he was paying homage to the gods.

Hanna nodded harder this time. Courage started showing in her eyes.

The swaddle in her arms moved slightly, and a soft cry of a baby broke the silence. Hanna rushed to rock the baby gently while also singing lullabies in whispers to the child. "We will love this child like we love our own. And the bag with gold coins that our lady has given us will help with raising this child," Garlan stepped closer and caressed the baby's head. But his eyes noticed that Hanna suddenly grew much more somber.

"Hanna? What is it?" he patted his wife's shoulder.

Hanna heaved and shook her head. "I just-I just cannot even fathom the pain in our lady's heart to have to ... to have to do this ..." the woman shivered and could not continue her sentence because her emotion brewed stronger.

The baby's cry subsided and Garlan remained quiet because he was not sure what the right thing to say was. His right hand still caressed the baby's head for a few more seconds before stopping and pulling his hand back to him as gentle as he could.

When the baby had settled a bit more, and the couple continued walking again. Once in a while they looked back to make sure noone followed them, then walked again with great care and silence.

The night had grown late, the sky was clear with stars dotted the vast darkness. The forest was quiet, there was only the sound of the boots getting in and out of the snow.

Garlan and Hanna arrived at a clearing in the depth of the forest, a clearing the size of about two soccer fields. The two stood still for a moment, admiring the only tree that grew in the middle of the snow-covered clearing.

The tree was massive, about two times the size of a giant sequoia. Its ancient age could be seen by the dark, knotted, rough bark of the trunk—a trunk with diameter so big that maybe fifty or more adults could join their hands and may still not be able to completely encircle it. The trunk was long with no branch whatsoever until up higher at which point the branches started showing and they were also impressive in sight.

"The enchanted tree," Garlan whispered with awe in his eyes.

"Look, the door ..." Hanna cocked her chin to the tree, to a spot on the tree where the gigantic roots intertwined as if they were forming a gate, and beyond the intertwining roots, on the trunk itself, was a door. A half-circle sturdy oak door painted blood red with a gold carving of a dragon in the middle of it. There were also some writings below the dragon carving, writing of characters carved in gold as well.

Garlan nodded. "Come, Hanna, let's walk again," he said and started walking across the clearing, straight to the red door with Hanna following close behind.

When the couple got to the front of the door, the two were quiet again.

"Where is the key that our lady gave to you?" Hanna whispered to her husband as her arms unconsciously tightened her embrace of the baby.

Garlan took something out of his coat pocket. A gleaming silver key. "It is here."

Hanna's expression grew more determined. "Do it, Garlan."

Suddenly a loud roar was heard from far away, a roar loud enough to rattle the red oak door. Garlan and Hanna startled and turned around to the direction of the roar. Their breathing became faster as fear crept within them.

"They have grown so restless these days. I hope all will be well again in our homeland here, Hanna." Garlan bit his lips as creases of worry deepened on his forehead.

"They are in a great pain and sorrow, Garlan. They are grieving the death of our beloved king, their master. I hope our lady can heal them ..." Hanna sighed before continuing,"Maybe the gods are indeed angry. It is a bad omen," she whispered with obvious tremble in her voice while her eyes focused on the baby in her embrace."Bad omen ..." she whispered again, now to the baby.

Roaring sound shook them again.

Then the two stood still for a moment as their heart became more weary by the sound of the roaring from far away.

"We have to go!" Garlan snapped himself back to the moment, turned to face the red door again, and placed the key into the key hole. His right hand was too shaky to get the key into the keyhole the first time. He tried a couple more times and was successful finally.

The key turned, and the red door creaked open.

Garlan heaved a loud sigh. Wafting fog came out from behind the door and the door creaked open wider.

Garlan took his wife's left hand, grasped it tight, and waited for the door to be completely open.

"This is it," Hanna tightened her right arm around the baby and her left hand grasped her husband's hand as tight as she could. She was scared, and she knew Garlan too.

When the door completely opened, they saw a tunnel and a light at the end of the tunnel. The couple stole a glance at each other and walked into the tunnel, a tunnel that would bring them to a world unknown for them.

The red door slammed shut behind them.

The gold carving of the writings on the door gleamed, it said:

This is the tree of the god Pan, a gift to the House of Evara for their service to him. May the majestic House of Evara be known forever as the House of the Dragon Healer.

Chapter 2

Chester was being so difficult today. She took him on his favourite route along the park and let him sniff on his own pace in the forest area behind the park.

She gave him extra cookies.

She let him roll around on the snow at the soccer field close by his home.

But he still pulled on his leash. A lot.

Chester, her newest client, a cream-colored golden retriever, was not a puppy anymore, he was two and a half. He passed his puppy training class, but he still had a hard time with leash or harness. It did not even matter what she did to help him calm down. Everything was worthy of sniffing and sniffing he would though that meant pulling his leash a lot, the slightest noise of wind breeze or car passing by would excite him to the point of leash pulling to check on the noise source. Stopping and munching on the snow was his thing to do now that it had snowed a lot the past few days.

"I need to chat with Lizzie about you, sweetie," Alanna scratched Chester's exposed belly when they arrived back at his home, a duplex he shared with his owner, Lizzie, and Lizzie's mom. Chester wriggled about, let out a panting sound, his mouth opened wide and he seemed to give a cheeky smile at Alanna. Some snow stuck on his nose and snow jacket and Alanna gently wiped them away.

Alanna laughed and rubbed his tummy even more, Chester let out a soft bark. "You are a naughty cutiepie, aren't you?" she rubbed Chester's hanging ear. Chester barked once again and this time Alanna smiled and stopped scratching him. She glanced at her watch. Almost 6PM. Chester's neighbour three doors down, Maddy, a ten-year-old feisty dachshund, was her next client.

Suddenly she let out a groan while holding her head. "Oh no ... not now," she whispered to herself. Her headache was back, the kind of pain that made her feel like there were wasps who were busy stinging the inside of her skull and took away the strength of her muscles to stand. She went to the doctor twice in the past three months to check about the headache. They found nothing that could be causing it.

The headache began about four months ago, and she had no idea how and why it started on her. She had never had any health issues. Until now. It got worse the past couple weeks. It came without warning, and the frequency had been getting more often. She knew it was not good if that headache attacked her during her walks with the dogs, but she could not tell the clients yet. She had to make sure what it was and she could not afford to lose her clients. The dogs were always safe because she had not walked them next to busy streets these days, just at the big park and the forest behind it. She just needed to sit down a bit and let the dogs cuddle close to her when the headache attack happened.

Now she just sat crosslegged on the porch with Chester sitting next to her. She massaged her temple and that helped a little. The torture usually lasted for about two-three minutes before subsiding by itself.

After her headache subsided, she took a deep breath, kissed Chester, and rang the doorbel of Lizzie's house, and Lizzie's wheelchair-bound mom answered. The mom could not handle Chester's energy while on a walk, that was why Lizzie paid Alanna, a dogwalker, to walk Chester two times a day while she worked.

After giving Lizzie's mom update on Chester, Alanna ran to her next client.

Maddy barked much more than Chester, but was much easier on the leash. She barked at other dogs or anything else that moved that were larger in size than her, and that was a lot given that she was a dachshund.

After Maddy's walk was done, Alanna rushed back to her own home—an apartment she shared with Dad and Mom.

She was a third year student majoring in psychology in university and had been working as a dogwalker the past year to save money to pay for the application fees for graduate schools and for the tests needed to complete her application package. She planned to apply for ten schools with some of the best programs in cognitive psychology, with luck and a good application package, she would stand a chance to be accepted to most of them. Two schools she had chosen as her "shooting for the sun" category, aka. near impossible-to-get-in-but-hey-why-not-try. So, she would have a busy year next year with all the applications.

Dad worked as a carpenter, and Mom was a homebaker known for her honey pecan cake and fruit-infused milk beverage—she helped Mom manage her homebaked goods business social media as well.

They had earned enough to give her a comfortable childhood as a single child. But the past two years had been stressful because Dad started having problems with arthritis which made it more challenging for him to do his carpentry work, while Mom had been having nightmares almost every night, and she had been unable to sleep well.

Alanna had been trying her best to take over some of Mom's duties at home, at the same time maintaining her 3.98 GPA at university and keeping up with the growth of her dogwalking business.

Her clients had been happy with her and recommending her service to their friends dan families. She was good with dogs, she knew that. She had always loved animals, and they loved her. Squirrels would come to her, birds and butterflies would fly around her, dogs would calm down and lay down with their belly exposed to her, a sign of complete trust, even the most aloof cats would come to her and want to be cuddled. Her own childhood dog, a black labrador named Lola, died last year at the ripe age of 17 and she cried for weeks.

She hoped she could continue her dogwalking business even after she started her grad school journey. It was just relaxing for her, to walk her client dogs or her beastie besties as she would call them.

When she got home, Mom and Dad were in the kitchen, talking in low voice. They were so engrossed in their conversation that they did not even realize Alanna was home.

"We cannot use them all up now. It's for her future too ..." Mom spoke with her back to Dad. She was busy preparing a big batch of honey pecan cake.

"Graduate school is expensive, I think we should chip in whatever we could ..." Dad sighed loudly while massaging his wrist.

"How about if ... if ... she has to go back? Will she still be able to go to the grad school like what she has been dreaming all these times then?" Mom's voice cracked.

Alanna turned cold. Go back where?

Alanna still stood in the hallway trying to eavesdrop a bit. An uneasy feeling tugged her from the inside. Her parents seemed to have been doing this a lot these days: Whispering and discussing things and completely shutting down when she walked in on them. At night when they thought she was already asleep, she could hear intense discussions in whispered voice from their bedroom next to hers. She knew it was always about her because faintly she could catch her name being mentioned. They also mentioned names like Garlan and Hanna, which she had no idea who they were. Mom was Diana Smith, and Dad was James Smith. She was Alanna Smith.

She knew that her parents were worried about her, about her future, about their own health, and that was normal for parents to do that. But what made her uneasy, and thought that there was a secret her parents had been keeping from her, was the way they looked at her.

They looked at her with such sadness as if they had to say goodbye to her soon. A few times Mom would just rush and hug her tight while holding back tears. When she asked her what was wrong, she just caressed her cheek and said nothing, I just love you so much, Alanna. I don't want to ever lose you. Strange but Alanna did not have the heart to keep pushing her parents for a better answer.

Mom and Dad had no more contact with their own family, they met at an orphanage as a child, kept in touch as they grew up in different adoptive families, and when things did not go well with their respective adoptive families, they got together when they were 18 and got married. That was it, that was what she had heard from her parents. That was how Alanna had grown up without grandparents and cousins. In light of this condition, Alanna could understand why her parents were worried about losing her, their only world.

Alanna took a deep breath and decided to stop eavesdropping. She loved her parents so very much, and she could not do this to them. Eavesdropping.

She went into the kitchen, and sure enough, her parents startled, Mom dropped her batter-covered spatula, and Dad haphazardly tried to find something to clean on the kitchen table.

"Mom, Dad, what is it?" she asked slowly.

"Alanna ..." Mom's mouth was half open. "No ... nothing ..."

Dad shook his head, backing Mom up.

"Listen you guys, you can tell me your concern, ok? We are family, aren't we? What is it? Money? I save some if you need it. I have a couple new clients, Chester starting since last week, and Bella starts tomorrow. I have extra."

"No, no! Please ... not that," Dad shook his head harder.

"What is it then? I know you have been keeping secrets from me," Alanna stared at both of them. Unblinked. She wanted to know why her parents had been keeping something from her.

Her parents glanced at each other, and in thousands of words that were exchanged in that glance, they decided not to tell her anything. They smiled a wry smile, shook their head in unison at her. "Please, Alanna, do not worry. It's just ... the regular things that parents worry about their daughter. You know ... do the dogs behave well with you? Do you get too cold going around in the snow everyday for hours with the dogs?" Dad answered.

"How is your healing journey?" Mom spoke with a soft gaze at her.

Alanna felt her stomach churning. "Healing from what?" she tried to be lighthearted, grabbing a piece of freshly-baked oatmeal cookie from the jar and popped it whole in her mouth.

"From Jake ..." Dad was careful.

Alanna stopped chewing her cookie. "Jake is the past. Truly. Six months is more than enough to heal from a broken heart. He decided to cheat, that's his problem. I don't need a man in my life now," she shrugged while busy cleaning cookie crumbs that fell out from her mouth to her sweater.

Dad and Mom glanced at each other again, and Alanna knew they were relieved. She was not that girl who cried in Mom's arms for hours when she broke off her relationship with Jake after his suggestive photos were found online by a friend of hers, who was friend with the girl he was cheating Alanna with.

Jake, her first ever "love." They dated for almost a year. She was never that interested in dating before Jake, a member of the campus' squash team. She was just busy with her volunteering at animals' shelter, her classes, her books, her friends, her beastie besties ...

"Alanna?"

"Stupid Jake," Alanna muttered in response to Mom's calling her.

"Sweetheart, we are just glad you have coped well with the breakup," Mom stepped closer to her.

Dad stepped closer to her, staring at her with an almost fleeting gaze, like he was in a state of awe of her.

"If only Jake knows who you actually are. He would be sorry to ever cheat on you ... so very sorry," he said in a low voice, like a whispering of a secret.

"Yeah, Dad! I am a badass bitch who is good with dogs and could do mean statistical analyses but clueless in the kitchen!" Alanna managed to laugh at her own self-deprecating joke.

But Dad and Mom did not laugh. They were dead serious. Alanna shrugged.

No, she had not told Mom and Dad about her extreme headache attack. They knew that sometimes she had headache, but she always managed to make it look much less serious than what it actually felt for her. She had told them it was nothing, it was from the stress and lack of sleep. They believed her because she was indeed under a lot stress from her school application stuff and her dogwalking business. She was relieved they did not ask more about the headache. There was no need to add more worries for her parents. The headache was no big deal, she was not sick. She was sure of that.

Chapter 3

But her headache disagreed with her decision of not telling her parents about the severity of it.

That night, after dinner, she had a massive headache attack that caused her to drop a glass she was holding. The glass shattered on the floor while she fell on her knees on the floor with loud groan coming out from her mouth and her hands on her head. The headache was painful to the point that she could not breathe.

Dad and Mom rushed to her, kneeling and hugging her.

"Garlan, it is happening! Garlan! Our child ..." Mom was sobbing. Even in her fuzzy mind ravaged by headache, Alanna knew it was strange. Why did Mom call Dad Garlan? That is not his name! She panted and tried to sit up straight.

Dad was quiet but Alanna could see clear liquid streaming down his cheek.

"How long have you had this kind of headache, Alanna?" Dad whispered right next to her ear.

Alanna tried to breathe. Her headache subsided a bit. "A few months ... three ... or four ..." she gasped her answer.

Mom sobbed louder.

"Something bad is happening in Alathyr ... something with the dragons ..." Dad mumbled, though Alanna did catch the word dragons and she knew she had gone nuts from the headache.

"My nightmares ... and this headache ..." Mom's eyes widened in terror. "We have to go back, Garlan."

"Mom! Dad is not Garlan! Who is Garlan?" Alanna could not hold it anymore. "What are you guys talking about? Go back where?" her headache became less of her focus now as it had lightened after such a torturous storm. She managed to sit with her back leaning to the kitchen cabinet. Mom and Dad now also sat in front of her with a certain helpless look on their face. Both of them had damp cheeks and they trembled.

"Our time here may not be much longer, Alanna," Dad spoke with sorrow that stabbed Alanna deep in the heart.

"What do you guys mean? Mom, Dad, you guys are freaking me out. Seriously."

"The nightmares that your Mom has been having, and your headache are signs, Alanna. Signs that all is not alright in the place where we come from. Where you come from. That world is calling us, calling you back."

"I'm from here, from Oakridge. Where else ...?" Alanna struggled to close her mouth.

"Our kingdom, our homeland, Alanna. Your homeland ..." Dad stole a glance at Mom, and Mom nodded. Dad sighed,"Your homeland ... Alathyr."

There was an awkward few seconds of silence when Alanna massaged her forehead, rubbed her palms on her face in an effort to gather bits and pieces of her sanity, before speaking with a mix of wonder and confusion, "You guys are just being weird now. This is a prank, isn't it? What exactly do you mean I am from Alath ... Alathyr?" Alanna shook her head. "Seriously ... Alathyr ... where is that?! Stop it, both of you. You two are freaking me out now," she felt a certain annoyance, anger even, that here in her moment of being tormented by a headache, her parents decided it was a proper, fitting time to prank her.

Mom and Dad did not laugh nor did they break into one of those tadaaaaa gotcha! Moment. Their expression grew even more somber. They stole glance at each other, and nodded.

It was Dad who told her the whole story about who she was and what had happened. A story that definitely sounded too strange to be true, like something that Dad had plucked straight out of some fantasy novel.

The only thing that stayed the same about her was her name.

She was indeed Alanna.

But she was not the daughter of James and Diana Smith. She was not Alanna Smith.

Dad's real name was Garlan, and Mom was Hanna. They had no blood relation with her whatsoever.

None of them came from Oakridge, or from this country, or even this universe.

They all came, like what Dad had just said, from a kingdom far away. A kingdom called Alathyr.

Alathyr was a kingdom in a universe where gods and human beings mingled and lived in closer relation than in this universe where Alanna had grown up in.

Alathyr had earned a special spot in the heart of Pan, the god of wildlife, forest and mountains.

Many many centuries ago, Pan—a god with a human body from the waist up and a goat from the waist down, and horns on his head that looked like goat's horns—walked the forest and fell in love with a beautiful princess named Cille. Pan turned himself to be a human, and married Cille. They were happy until Zeus, the king of the gods, called Pan back to his duty and Pan had to leave Cille.

Cille, who was pregnant, gave birth to a boy that looked like a regular human being. The boy, named, Pryssus, was the one who then became the forefather and founder of the Alathyr Kingdom.

Pan felt bad for not being able to be present as a father to Pryssus, decided to grant his kingdom a great honour. The god of wilds, mountains, and nature decided to let Pryssus and his descendants in Alathyr be the caretakers of his beloved warriors and prized pets, the dragons.

There were four dragons that were entrusted to the House of Pryssus. These dragons were blessed with kindness and long life. They could be weakened, they could get injured and sick, but they would not die for a long, long, time. They also could not be turned to support evil as long as their master, the king or queen of Alathyr, remained in the path of goodness.

These dragons served as the ride of the gods when wars broke between the gods of the Olympus and the demons of the underworld, the followers of Erebus, the evil god of underworld. One of these dragons was also the ride of the king Alathyr. Thus the king of Alathyr was the guardian of the dragons, and the rider.

It was such a great honour for Alathyr to have these dragons in their care and guardianship.

Now Pan also chose one more family for a special treatment. The House of Evara, who was the house where his love Cille, was born into.

If the royal house of the Kings of Alathyr—House of Pryssus—became became the guardian of the dragons, with the king as the dragon rider, the House of Evara was the dragon healer. Only one healer in each generation that was chosen by the dragons themselves. The dragons showed their complete trust to this person by bowing their head to him/her, something that these proud beings would never do to just anyone.

Alanna's birthmother, Eilin, was a dragon healer.

Eilin was a reluctant healer at best. She was an adventurous, fiery, and stubborn woman. Having to stay always close to home and healing dragons were not her dream job. She was the kind of woman who followed her heart, and she did exactly that. She fell in love and eloped with a lowly guard of her family mansion, a man named Bragan. A man she had truly loved.

It became a horrendous scandal because as a dragon healer, her marriage had to be approved by the family council, and she was to be married to a man with similar social standing as her, not an orphan guard like Bragan.

Bragan and Eilin elopement was kept top secret. Tragically, Bragan was killed by an assassin sent by the father of Eilin.

Brokenhearted Eilin was three months pregnant by then. She threatened to commit suicide if her family made her abort her baby.

The dragons grew restless, as if they could sense the tragedy in their healer's life.

Finally it was decided that Eilin would be kept in a dungeon during her pregnancy. Her pregnancy was kept as a secret, so the cover story to everyone was that Eilin was sick because she spent too much time healing the dragons and made sure the magical beings were safe and happy.

Eilin gave birth to a baby girl named Alanna, and in a tragic coincidence that same night, the beloved king of the Alathyr, King Vilmos, died after an illness. His queen took the throne, as a throne caretaker until the crown prince, who was only a toddler then, was old enough to be the next king.

The family of Eilin believed that baby Alanna was a bad omen because she was born out of a forbidden love, without the consent of the family council, let alone their deity Pan. They did not even care to think about the fact that King Vilmos had been sick for some time.

They forced Eilin to give up the baby, and Eilin realized that the best chance for her daughter to have a somewhat normal, peaceful life was if she was away from her own mother, from the House of Evara. Thus after only a few minutes in her mother's arms, baby Alanna was given to Hanna, Eilin's most trusted chambermaid and her husband, the carpenter Garlan, to be brought to the door at the enchanted tree—a door which was an heirloom, a treasure of the House of Evara, a precious gift from Pan himself. Pan protected the door with his own spell to prevent those with an evil heart and dark intentions to ever pass through safely to the other side.

The door was a portal to another universe, and the heartbroken Eilin decided that was where her daughter had to be whisked away to. She just wanted a safe place for Alanna to grow up, without the mark as a bad omen.

With a sacred key that Eilin gave to them, Garlan and Hanna opened the door and brought Alanna to this universe, raising her without telling her her tragic true story ...

At that point, Alanna's jaw dropped. Her mind had blanked out.

"Alanna?" Mom patted her shoulder as gentle as she could.

Alanna heard Mom's calling, but her mind was one big jumbled mess right now. Her right palm was covering her open mouth.

"Alanna, please say something, sweetheart. We are so sorry that we did not tell you much earlier. I guess we have been trying to fool ourselves to think that we can always stay here. As a family," Dad's voice quivered.

"Do I really have to go back to ... Alathyr?" Alanna asked, and in her mind, all her plans, her dogwalking business, her grad school dreams, all shattered one by one. It was all just so callous.

Mom and Dad were quiet, and Alanna groaned when the headache came back.

Mom rushed to hold her tight, her rolling tears wet Alanna's hair when she sobbed.

"We have to. Your headache means the dragons are calling you. They are restless, and upset about something."

"Am I a dragon healer?" Alanna tightened her grab of her head. The headache did not subside.

"We have to bring you to the dragons to be sure, Alanna. Dad and I cannot be sure about it. The dragons decide for themselves."

Alanna cried when the pain made her whole body start convulsing.

"We are going. Tonight. This is not good. The pain could kill you!" Dad stood up with panic that started to color his expression.

But Alanna did not have any clarity of mind or strength to reply, she fell face first on the ground from her sitting position and started crying in pain. The headache felt like it was ripping her head apart.

And she heard voices.

Not really anyone talking or whispering anything to her, it was more like a murmur. Busy murmurs as if there were more than one person tried to contact her.

Except it was not the murmuring of human beings. She could tell that even with the brutal headache. It was heavier, lower voice than any human she ever heard. It sounded almost like a growl. Something, or someone, not human, that was trying to tell her something.

"I heard voices ... murmurs ... growling ...." She trembled, and she saw Mom and Dad look at each other. They understood what the murmurs were about.

"The dragons ... Alanna ... they are indeed calling for you," Dad nodded.

Her headached pounded her and she wailed and tried to pull her hair in a last ditch effort to reduce the pain. The murmurs disappeared when her headache took over her focus again.

"Let's go. Leave everything. We are taking her back to Alathyr!" Dad shouted in panic.

Alanna knew, she had no other choice.

Chapter 4

Mom and Dad had to wait a bit till her headache subsided because she could not even stand when the pain ravaged her. She shivered and sobbed softly, and after a good five minutes, the pain subsided. Deep in her heart, Alanna knew the next wave of pain was coming again at a closer interval than at other days before now.

Mom helped her put on her jacket and snow boots.

When they were ready, they stepped out in the cold night air, and snow had started falling again. From the distance, Alanna could hear a few dogs barking. Her heart broke when she thought of all the dogs, her beastie besties, that would just suddenly lose their buddy. She would lose all her clients. She knew it. She had to come to their house, one by one, and apologize massively if she ever got a chance to come back here.

She would miss all her graduate school application deadlines.

She would lose contact with all her friends.

She would lose her life here. The only life she had ever known so far.

If I ever came back ... maybe I could rebuild my life here. That thought came to her.

"Do I really have to go?" she whispered as Mom led her to the back yard of their apartment complex, and they kept walking to a small forest behind the fence.

Dad turned to her. "We have to, Alanna. Your headache would only get much worse. The dragons are calling you."

"Where is that tree? The portal?" she got enough clarity of mind now to start questioning that logistical puzzle. Where would they find the enchanted tree with the door in the middle of it?

Her parents, her adopted parents, did not answer.

They kept walking and snowfall became heavier and heavier.

They got to a small grass clearing in the middle of the forest.

"It is here," Dad nodded.

"Where? It's just snow and dead trees here!" Alanna looked around.

Dad took something out of his jacket pocket. Mom stepped closer to Alanna and grasped her hand.

Alanna could see what Dad now had in the clasp of his hand. A gleaming silver key. The key was big compared to other key Alanna had seen in her life. The bow of the key was carved in beautiful, intricate silver carving.

"Are you ready?" Dad stared at both Mom and Alanna. Nobody nodded, and Dad sighed before turning around, standing still for a moment, and letting snowflakes fall on him, little white dots started covering his short wavy grey hair.

His body shook like a twig in the wind, and suddenly he just looked so frail, so timid in the face of whatever it was that he had to do now.

After another long deep breath, Dad kneeled and stabbed the key on the snowy ground.

Mom hugged Alanna's shoulder and Alanna just stood stiff, unblinked, trying to not miss any event that may happen now.

And it was as if there had always been a curtain there in the middle of the clearing, a clearing that Mom and Dad had always discouraged her to go to in the past. It is too dark, too quiet, too muddy, too ... was what they had told her.

The curtain, invisible, but must have been there indeed because as it opened, a tree started to appear behind it.

"What the ..." Alanna struggled to say something. Fu*k was the natural thing to say to complete that phrase but she was too absorbed with her visual experience she just let the sentence hang there.

A tree. Massive. It looked ancient with dark, knotted, rough bark of the trunk. The trunk was long with no branch whatsoever until up higher at which point the branches started showing and they were knotted and twirled to each other.

She had never seen a tree so massive, so ancient like that.

Indeed there was a door in the middle of the tree. The door was at the point where the gigantic roots of the tree intertwined as if they were forming a gate. Beyond the intertwining roots, on the trunk itself, that was where the door was located. A half-circle sturdy oak door painted blood red with a gold carving of a dragon in the middle of it. There were also some writings below the dragon carving, writing of characters carved in gold as well.

"Our god Pan's tree ..." whispered Mom to Alanna.

"It's crazy ... Mom ... how come I never knew there was a tree there?" she whispered back.

"Your sight is shielded from it by its sorcery, Alanna. The key opened it."

"Sorcery ... Mom, this is nuts," she trembled.

Mom did not listen to her anymore.

Dad walked to the tree, and Mom walked behind him.

"Dad! Mom! Wait!" she shouted, "Are you guys sure it's not dangerous?" she asked in exasperation. Mom would go all ballistic if Alanna crossed the road without looking left and right and left, and now she walked without any hesitation to a massive tree who had just appeared in front of her.

Dad and Mom did not seem to hear her.

Alanna reluctantly followed, and the closer she walked to the tree, the stranger she felt the atmosphere around it. The cold winter air seemed to intensify, and the intense smell of forest filled her nostrils.

And the murmurs started again, this time it was louder than the last time she heard it. Hissing and murmuring filled her ears and she dropped down on the snow, covering her ears with both hands.

"Alanna!" her parents rushed back to her.

"The murmuring ... is so loud now!" she gasped.

"Come! We have to open the door! We have to go home! The dragons are calling you. Something has happened in Alathyr!"

Dad helped her stand, and she could hear faint sobbing from Mom direction.

She stood, her legs shook like they were made of jelly, but Dad grabbed her waist and helped her walk the rest of the distance to the red door on the tree.

"You have been having the headaches for months now, that means Alathyr has been trying to call you back all this time. The dragons finally also call you through their voices!" Mom sobbed. "I hope all is alright in Alathyr," Mom continued.

"I am opening the door," Dad announced when all three stood in front of the red door.

Mom nodded, and Alanna shook her head to try to do away with the murmuring that seemed to live within her skull now.

"Be strong, Alanna," Mom took her hand, and Dad inserted the key to the keyhole.

The key turned with creaking sound, and all was quiet.

Snow kept falling, and Alanna shivered from the cold and the anxiety.

The red door creaked, slowly but surely, open.

Tears streamed down Alanna's cheek. She did not think much actually, that logical analytical part of her brain seemed to have shut down. At this point she was just sad and shocked. She was maybe angry too—how could her parents just uproot her like this? Is this some kind of a sick, elaborate joke?

Who, and what awaits me behind that door? She asked herself. But she'd rather not know the answer now because she would just bolt and run as fast as she could, away from her parents, the red door, and Alathyr. But she could not just run away. She could not do it to her parents, her adoptive parents. They did not have much choice either. Garlan and Hanna had been, and were fantastic parents to her. They had done a very good job in carrying out their task of protecting her, raising her well.

The headache and murmuring were not to be taken lightly, she had experienced the intensity of their attack, and she did not want to die because of them.

Mom took her left hand, and Dad her right hand, and guided her to enter the room behind the door when the door was open.

She walked in slow steps, she could not will herself to walk fast.

The murmuring got quieter, and that gave her a relief.

Behind the door was a tunnel, about twenty meters long. There was a bright light at the end of the tunnel.

The red door slammed close behind them, and the only source of light in the tunnel was the light at the end of it. Alanna could feel cold wind in there, all was dark around her. She could not see what the tunnel was made of, though she could feel like she was walking on a damp ground.

At first she thought she was hallucinating, but she did not. She could hear sounds in the tunnel. Sound of bird chirping, water flowing, leaves rustling, gentle breeze blowing that brought fragrance of spring flowers with it.

"Do you hear it, Mom? Dad? Smell it?" she whispered.

"The sounds and smells of nature?" Mom glanced at her with a smile.

"This is Pan's tunnel. He is the god of nature, of wilds and forests. A gentle god. He makes sure that this tunnel could be passed freely and safely only by those who have the key from the House of Evara, and those who have good intentions in their heart," Dad explained.

Alanna nodded. Pan. The god that began all her life's weirdness now.

Mom and Dad fell to silence again.

Alanna tried to breathe slower though it was a struggle. But at least Pan seemed like a kind, gentle god. Not one of those monstrous, always-pissed-off type that she had read in mythology books.

The walk across the tunnel was strange at best. Alanna felt like time passed differently in there, she felt sleepy, then rejuvenated, and sleepy again, all within the little walk.

When they got to the end of the tunnel, there was another door. This one was also red, and rays of light came from behind it.

"We are here. We are in Alathyr," Dad spoke with clear shiver in his voice.

Mom nodded. "We are back home."

Chapter 5

Alanna watched as Dad opened the door, and cold wind blew from outside. She was startled by how cold it was.

Dad turned around and looked at both Alanna and his wife. "Ready?" he whispered.

Mom nodded, while Alanna was undecided, though she was leaning toward No.

They got out from the door one by one. Dad, Mom, and Alanna.

It was also winter in Alathyr.

The three of them now stood in a snow-covered clearing, with the enchanted tree stood as the only tree in the middle of the clearing.

Snow was thick, and the tall branches of the enchanted tree were covered in snow, as did its twigs and trunk.

Alanna took a deep breath, and the cold air that rushed to fill her lungs brought with them a certain sense of familiarity, something that surprised her at first. The air felt lighter, cold, but light. She could also smell faint fragrant of trees, most likely from the forest that surrounded this clearing.

"Is it almost sunset?" Mom looked up to the grey sky.

"Looks like it," Dad answered.

Alanna was quiet, she would not even venture to guess how much time difference exist between here and her universe. Though winter there was also winter here. But were they in the same year?

"Your home, Alanna," Mom grabbed Alanna's elbow and twisted her arm around it.

"We have to go to find our lady Eilin," Dad started moving. "It gets dark soon!"

"Eilin ..." Alanna repeated the name. She just could not get used to the whole idea that she was ... well ... she was not Alanna like she thought she had known all these years.

"Your mother. The one who gave birth to you," Mom turned and patted her shoulder gently.

"This is nuts. Mom, I don't know if I can ..."

"Yes you can. You can do this. It is time. It is for your own good. Do you still hear the murmuring voice? Or the headache?"

Alanna paused, and shook her head. There was a clear relief in Mom and Dad's expression, as if a weight had been lifted off their shoulder.

"I hope I haven't been such a big burden to you guys," Alanna spoke again, she was not sure why she said that, but the relief in her adoptive parents face made her feel slightly uneasy. Has she been a burden? A glitch in their plan for the future? A roadblock for them in reaching their own dreams, dreams they have to put aside because they are given a task to raise a child who is not even their own? Alanna felt sadness that she could not explain because it just seeped into every fiber of her being, like she was unwanted.

Mom and Dad turned to her, their eyes widened in surprise.

"Alanna! Of course not! You were not, are not, and never will be a burden to us. We love you since the first moment we met you," Mom grabbed her shoulder.

"We have been married for some years when our lady Eilin asked us to help her raise you. We prayed for a child, but the gods never granted us this wish. Until you," this time Dad spoke, his expression grew much gentler.

"You are a gift to us, Alanna," Mom gazed into Alanna's eyes, and her lips trembled in an effort to not cry.

Alanna hugged Mom, she knew both of them needed it. "I am just so scared now, Mom. Can I still call you Mom? Dad?"

"We are your parents, not your birth parents but your parents nevertheless, Alanna. I am sure we can ask lady Eilin if it is alright you call us Mom and Dad still," Hanna turned to her husband, and Garlan nodded.

That was not a satisfying answer for Alanna. She could not just call another woman Mom. Her life was not a stage play where people could just change roles easily. Her life had been turned upside down, she was in a foreign land, and she was not about to lose her parents too—the parents she had known all these years.

She was going to say something when they heard noises from the direction of the forest.

The three of them turned to watch the source of the noise.

There were birds. Black and huge. They flapped their wings noisily, the noise they heard was the wings flapping and trees' twigs broke when they hit them.

"What the ..." Alanna's jaw dropped when she saw those big black birds.

The birds cawed. Their cawing was deafening and they flew closer.

"Crows! Big ones!" Mom screamed.

"They are not friendly! Run!" Dad grabbed Alanna's hand and pulled her.

"Crows are not that big!" Alanna shouted and ran along with Dad, Mom followed close behind.

"Just run!" Mom shouted.

Alanna looked back as she ran, and convinced herself that indeed those were crows, though they were three times the size of crows that she had encountered before in her life.

Running in snowy ground was not easy to say the least, and the cawing of the crows got so much louder the closer they got to them.

Her heart thumped hard as she ran with all her might, she fell once and Dad grabbed her to stand up again, and there with snow on her face, she ran again.

But they were not fast enough.

The first four crows got to them and loudly cawed as they started attacking the three people. Alanna looked up and saw glistening claws pointed down right at her and she screamed and instinctively shielded her face with her hands.

She fell on the snow, and she knew Mom and Dad too.

Then she heard whooshing sound as if something flew past her.

She kneeled on the snow with her head down and her arms shielded it. She kept shouting No, and shook her head. If her life ended like this, what an anticlimax it would be.

"Attack! Kill them all!" she heard a voice. It was not Mom or Dad.

She lifted her head, and saw a pair of round black eyes and black wings and sharp claws going for her face.

She screamed, and she saw something whooshing past her head, and the giant crow let out a loud shriek and fell on the ground with a thud. An arrow, black with white fur on the tip, had killed the crow with a direct stab in between its eyes.

An arrow that flew past a few centimeters from her head to hit the crow. If her head had moved just a tad bit just now in the wrong direction ...

Shiver went down her spine.

Then she saw more arrows flying above her, killing the coming crows with extreme precision. One by one the crows fell from the sky, their bodies scattered on the snowy ground like black spots on white surface.

Mom took her hand and she stood up albeit with shaky legs, and Dad stood in front of them.

"Who are they?" Mom shivered.

Dad did not answer, his focus was now on the group of men on other side of the clearing, at the mouth of the forest there. They ran closer to them now.

The men got to them, and Alanna could see them clearer.

They all wore simple clothes: Grey wool tunic, black belt, black pants and snow boots, grey cape, and grey hood that covered their head.

There were about ten men, they all looked fit, with tall solid body. It was obvious they were well trained, at least in archery. Possibly soldiers of some sort. They had identical bows and arrows, all black. The only one who had black arrows with white fur tip was the man who stood at the front of the group. Their leader. The one who had shot the arrow so precise that it had killed the crow who was going to attack Alanna without wounding her too. The leader was at least half a head taller than the rest of his men, with broad shoulders and chest, solid muscles the shape of which could be gleaned from beyond his simple thick tunic and cape.

"Who are you? Your clothes show that you are not from here. We have seen you came out from the tree of Pan," the leader spoke. His voice was deep and commanding. But it was his eyes that made Alanna lose focus on his question. The eyes were so blue, dark blue like the deep ocean. Beautiful big eyes, though there was no warmth there. His face was not handsome like celebrity model handsome, but he was definitely not bad looking either. His whole look was rugged, with stubby moustache and beard forming shadows around his chin and jaws. There was a black tattoo on the left side of his head, a tattoo that looked like a long, sharp claw that went from his left temple to his left jaw. His head was covered in grey hood, but Alanna could see straggling hair blown by the wind, wavy and dark. There was heaviness that was obvious in the leader's gaze, heaviness that mixed with a certain sadness and exhaustion.

"We are Garlan, Hanna, and our daughter Alanna. We are going to the House of Evara, to see our lady Eilin," Garlan did not tell who Alanna really was out of caution.

The leader tilted his head. "What business have you with Lady Eilin? Why did you all come out from the tree of Pan?"

Garlan gasped softly. "We are … our lady Eilin's helpers. Who are you?"

The leader looked up to the sky. "Your question will be answered later. It is almost dark and this place will swarm with those demon crows at night."

"Demon crows? Alathyr never has that kind of filth!" now Mom spoke.

The leader tilted his head in a mixture of confusion and amusement and he spoke in response to Mom, "I do not know where all of you have been at the past few months. But here is one thing for you to know now: Alathyr, the one you knew, is no more."

Chapter 6

A shock gasp escaped Mom's mouth, and so did Dad. Alanna just froze, trying to process the fact that her homeland, the kingdom that they had planned to bring her to, to go home to, was no more.

The leader of the group stared at Dad unblinked and continued, "You still have not answered my question about why and how you came out from Pan's tree."

Dad straightened up his back and answered loud enough for everyone to hear,"I will answer that only if you take me to meet Lady Eilin!"

The men behind the leader stirred, some of them tightened their grasp on their bow, it was obvious they were not pleased with the way Dad talked to their leader.

The air around grew tense and heavy. Alanna must admit she was proud of Dad now. His thin bony back stood up against the men, solid and tall with their bows and arrows. I hope we don't get killed though, Alanna whispered in her mind.

It was obvious things had changed a lot in Alathyr, whatever the changes were, if it involved the presence of demon crows, it must not have been good.

The leader stared at Dad, then Mom, and when his eyes rested on Alanna, Alanna could have sworn she would go into panic mode. His gaze lingered for a moment on Alanna before he lifted his right palm, a sign for his followers to scale down their response and to de-escalate the tension, then he took a deep breath, "You have come out from the tree of Pan, and noone with bad intentions would survive it. It means you can be trusted. We will take you to our dragon healer, Lady Eilin."

Dad sighed a visible long breath of relief, Mom too. Alanna just froze. All was just too weird for her now.

"We have to go!" the leader turned around and walked away fast, members of his group followed him, some of them waited and let Alanna and her parents walked first before they followed behind them.

Alanna tried her best to keep up. Snow started falling again and the winter jacket she wore was not enough to keep her warm now. Winter here just felt so much colder than in her universe.

The headache was back.

Alanna panted as she tried to withstand the pounding pain within her skull. Mom knew what was happening when Alanna fell and kneeled on the snow. Her hands grabbed both sides of her head.

"Stop! My daughter is in pain!" Mom screamed.

The leader stopped, turned around and rushed to them.

"The dragons ... are calling her. She has been having these horrible headache," Dad whispered carefully.

The leader, whose name was still not known by Alanna, kneeled in front of Alanna. "We have to reach our hideout,

Lady Eilin and the dragons are there. The closer she is to the dragons, the better she would feel. Is that it?" the leader looked to Dad for an answer.

Dad and Mom nodded in harmony.

Alanna groaned again. The pain turned sharp, it felt like some bees were busy stinging her skull from the inside.

"We have to rush, the sun has set and those demon crows fly here at night. Would it be alright if I carry you?" the leader looked around and asked the question. Alanna was not sure she heard it correctly, she shook her head. "I don't even know your name," she groaned and her headache was getting more intense.

"Is that really important? Tristan. That's my name. Now I will carry you. We have to rush!" he said out loud his name, Mom and Dad looked at each other with their eyebrows furrowed. Alanna did not have much time to process that, she tried to stand one more time and fell down again.

Alanna gave up. Tristan easily lifted and carried her.

They walked again, faster and faster as darkness fell around them. Alanna just focused on trying to breathe with pain that ravaged her entire head, though she could also heard faint heartbeats of Tristan. The coldness of winter that had stung her because her winter jacket and gloves did not seem to be enough was by now reduced by her closeness to Tristan's body.

At some point, Alanna felt better and requested to walk by herself again, to which Tristan complied.

Tristan led the way, and they walked on what felt to Alanna like zigzag route, along the underbrushes, across thre small frozen river, and they got to the end of the river where there was a frozen waterfall.

The waterfall was silvery in the light of the moon, glistening and beautiful in all its frozen jagged shape. It was one tall waterfall, maybe about the height of a two coconut trees stacked on top of each other. The gleaming silver frozen waterfall caught Alanna's full attention. She had to gasp for air when she took in the beauty of the waterfall.

"I can't believe I see this. This must be Knyra, the waterfall that everyone knows it exists but nobody knows the location," whispered Mom right at her ear, her voice quivered from the cold and from the astonishment that she must have felt at this moment, engulfing her and forcing her brain to believe what her eyes had seen.

"So ...beautiful, Mom," she whispered back, her mouth had been half open since the moment she saw the frozen waterfall.

"I have never been here before, Alanna. I used to think this waterfall was just a myth. People of Alathyr know it exists, but strangely nobody could tell you where it is. The only waterfall in Alathyr!" Mom had not taken her eyes off Knyra.

Alanna turned her head quickly to Mom, she found the whole explanation strange. How could people know it existed, the only waterfall in Alathyr, but noone knew its location?

"Come!" Tristan shouted. The men had finished checking around the perimeter area to make sure there was noone else there but their group.

Alanna decided to put aside her question about Knyra and followed Mom and Dad who had walked in front of her.

They walked on a small pathway that led to the rocky hill that formed the backdrop of the waterfall. The frozen pathway was slippery so they had to walk in a single file, holding onto protruding rocks that for untrained eyes may have seemed like random rocks, but they were actually positioned in such a way that people could grab them as they walked in the small pathway.

When they got to the hill area behind the waterfall, Tristan took a small dagger, and stabbed the dagger at a small opening that looked just like a crack in between two rocks, one of many such cracks there on the rocky wall behind the waterfall. One needed to know which one of these many cracks was the correct crack to insert the dagger.

Alanna heard a thumping sound, and she was shocked to see a part of the rocky wall opened, like a door.

The rock creaked open from right to left. Mom and Dad were like Alanna, in awe of what was happening in front of them.

When the rock door was completely open, the group went inside, and Mom had to pull Alanna's hand.

Nobody said anything, anything at all, about what a crazy place that was! A place behind rocky hill, a space behind the waterfall!

Alanna walked inside. There was a long corridor, like a tunnel cave that smelled like water and mud, and they all had to walk in single file again. Torches hung on the left and right side of the cave provided much needed lighting.

The corridor went downhill, and they kept walking until they saw the light at the end of the corridor.

There was a metal gate, about two meters high, fully welded in intricate details, and two guards were posted there.

The two guards nodded their head in full respect at Tristan.

"His Majesty the King is back!" one of them shouted to those who were behind the gates—an announcement of sort.

Alanna felt lightheaded. His Majesty the King.

That guy was the king, the one who had carried her halfway here.

"That was what we thought when we heard what his name was just now. The king was just a three year old boy when you were born and taken by us to another universe, Alanna," Mom whispered at her.

But Alanna was too busy looking around to give any reply to Mom.

They had walked into a cavernous hall beyond the metal gate. The hall was a mix of nature and human-made. It was a cavernous cave, and humans had then further carved it, made it into a huge space for dwelling and layers of catacombs like structure.

The rock that formed the whole underground structure was blackish-reddish, looked ancient indeed.

"What is this place?" Alanna asked herself the question.

"It ... it looks like an underground hideout, hidden behind the Knyra," Dad answered her with little certainty. "Knyra ... and this ... it's ... it's ..." Dad failed to finish his sentence.

Alanna nodded mindlessly. Her eyes were too busy scanning the whole cavernous rock hall. Her mind was not with her parents. Or her headache which by now had completely disappeared. Or Tristan. Or King Tristan.

There were people in the hall. From the way they looked, they were all soldiers, though there were some women and children and elderly as well. They came in and out from the various corridors around the hall that led to more corridors.

It was a massive catacomb. An underground structure of massive proportion. She decided that by now.

She felt like she was just floating in a room, all noises died down and she was just in awe.

Until she heard roaring.

She startled and was back on her feet and her reality here.

"Dragons," whispered Dad to her with awe in his voice.

Roars of several dragons, loud and heavy and soul-shattering.

"Please let Lady Eilin know, there are guests for her here!" Tristan—who had been busy receiving reports from his men in the cave—gave an order, and a soldier ran to one of the corridors to get Lady Eilin. Tristan left the company after that.

Roaring of the dragons shook the hall again, they seemed to come from behind the hall. Somewhere down one of the corridors.

Alanna's heart beat fast, she was nervous and unsure of what to say or to do. Her birth mother, a dragon healer from the House of Evara, someone who had decided to let her go when she was a newborn. What did she look like? What did she sound like? What should she call her? Mom too? That would be so strange ...

"Alanna ... my daughter ..." someone called her, and Alanna let out a soft gasp, startled, and turned around.

She saw her. Lady Eilin.

A woman in her forties, tall and slender, with large, warm honey-coloured eyes and light brown hair tinted with the greyness of the aging process. She was beautiful, and a certain aura of calmness, but also of intelligence and bravery exuded from her. She did not wear skirt, but long flowy grey pants with silver belt, and red long-sleeve wool tunic. Her hair was bundled in one bundle on top of her head. Her skin was pale and wrinkles started showing around her eyes and lips. Her whole body exuded flowery fragrance—a mix of lily and jasmine.

Alanna froze. My birth mother, was all she could tell herself in her mind.

"My lady!" Mom and Dad kneeled on the ground to show full respect to Eilin. Alanna stood still, she was not about to kneel because she was just so, so confused.

But Lady Eilin did not seem to hear them. Her attention was only on Alanna. She rushed to stand in front of Alanna, extended her arms to hug her daughter, but Alanna took a few steps back.

"No ... no ... this is too ... weird," Alanna shook her head and tears streamed on her cheek. That woman there was still a stranger for all she cared, though she was told that she was her birth mother.

"I am your mother, sweet Alanna," Eilin's voice cracked from her own sobbing.

"I am 22 years old this year. I have lived a completely different life until just ... just moments ago. How? How do I adjust to live in this place? With you, with these people?" Alanna spoke fast, questions in her heart, all blurted out. "I have plans with my life! Not this!" she cried. "You gave me away!" that one last sentence had been like a thorn in Alanna's heart. She knew Lady Eilin had to do that, but still the pangs of pain refused to leave her alone.

Lady Eilin shook and started sobbing too, and she spoke in between her sobs, "I had to! I want you to have a safe, happy life somewhere where you are not seen as the bad omen!"

Alanna stood still. Her brain sputtered to process Eilin's words.

"There is not a day, not a day, pass that I do not think of you, my daughter. I kneel before the gods everyday to pray for your happiness, Alanna."

That alone sent Alana into crying fits because she could not deny one thing: How much Lady Eilin looked like her.

All of a sudden the dragons' roar shook the hall again.

Lady Eilin wiped her tears, and nodded at Alanna, "They can smell you are here. They want to see you," she said with a tender smile.

Chapter 7

Alanna could not decide if she would go and see the dragons. She stood and was just busy wiping her tears.

Lady Eilin took a step closer to her, nodded her head. "Come, Alanna. I promise they are not scary."

"I have never, ever, thought dragon was real. It's too crazy!" she shook her head when her brain failed to give her any consoling explanation.

"Come," it was now Mom, the Mom she had known all these times, who took her hand and she followed when Mom guided her to follow Lady Eilin.

Lady Eilin walked first, followed by Mom, Alanna, and Dad. They went to the rock corridor that was directly in front of them, the corridor led to a rock staircase that was small and only fitted one person. The staircase was long and it wound down for some time, going much lower than the level where the entrance to the underground cavernous hall was. Spiderwebs hung thick and low, brushing Alanna's face and she was busy trying to wipe away the sticky strands.

Roaring of the dragons shook the staircase—the staircase that was already ancient with steps that were not the same height and made of rough rocks. This time the roar sounded much closer, and that rattled Alanna even more.

She stopped on her track just to manage her breathing that became faster and faster, while her hands got colder and colder. Then she walked again after Dad gently nudged her.

They got to the bottom of the winding stairs and saw light at the end of a short tunnel.

Lady Eilin who walked at the front, now turned around and found Alanna with her gaze. "Are you ready, Alanna?" her voice was melodious. She tilted her head slightly and waited for an answer.

Mom and Dad stood to the left and right of Alanna, and both stared at her now with anticipation.

Alanna knew she had not much choice. At least if she could go back to her own universe she had a great story to tell: To see dragons and live to tell about it! Nothing could beat that.

With small, shaky steps, Alanna followed Lady Eilin to enter yet another cavernous hall. The massive hall shaped like a rocky dome without a closed roof because right at the top was an opening, from which Alanna could see the sky, far far above. Could it be for the dragons to fly out? That thought crossed Alanna's mind.

The dragons were there.

Four of them.

They were wondrous creature, with black-gold scales and two smooth, glistening sharp horns. They had a pair of large wings, sharp claws, and red eyes with golden pupils, thick black eyelashes, and they stared at everyone in front of them with full focus. Their teeth were sharp, like canine teeth, their saliva dripped as they breathed out loud. The height of the tallest dragon was maybe about ten meters or so, and the rest was just a tad bit shorter.

"They are-are real ... shit ..." Alanna fought to maintain some semblance of control over her shock. She failed as her knees shook, her mouth opened wide, and her eyes stared unblinked at the four dragons.

"Anthor, the northern dragon also the oldest, biggest, and tallest one. Anthor is also his majesty the king's ride. Selivor, the southern dragon is the twin of Drathor, the eastern dragon, and the youngest of them all and the only girl, Rannathor, the western dragon. Four corners of the wind, four dragons," Lady Eilin introduced the dragons just like she did with friends. She nodded her head to them one by one and stated their name. Anthor, Selivor, and Drathor nodded their large head back at Eilin while maintaining a regal stand. It was the girl dragon Rannathor who let out a loud groan, her large eyes winked a few times in some sort of playful glint, and opened her mouth wide as if she was smiling at Alanna.

Alanna fell on her knees. She could not hold herself up anymore. Four dragons stood proudly in front of her. She had never thought too much about dragons before in her life, in fact Garlan and Hanna, her parents so far, never really mentioned it in a special way. Now they were in front of her. Mythical beasts that were not so mythical afterall.

"My dear friends, Anthor, Selivor, Drathor, and sweet Rannathor ... I bring my daughter here. Her name is Alanna. In her veins flow the blood of Evara, the foreignness that you smell in her because she has been through the door of Pan to another universe, and back here ..." Lady Eilin turned to Alanna and smiled at her, then she turned to the dragons again, "She is not a dragon healer yet. You will have to decide if she is whom you will trust."

Alanna shook her head. She wanted to go to grad school, to do research on psychology, not a dragon healer. She was a dogwalker, not a dragon healer.

The dragons were quiet, their eyes trained on Alanna and that made her wish the earth would just swallow her right there and then.

Then Alanna heard a soft purr, and she turned to see from which dragon that was.

The girl. Rannathor. She now tilted her head to the side and walked closer to Alanna. Alanna decided then that the dragon's walk was so similar to the walk of a T-Rex dinosaur. When Alanna was a little girl, she went on fullblown obsessive mode on dinosaurs. She had learned so much about these prehistoric beasts that she could tell right now: Dragons were just T-Rex-looking beasts that possibly could fly because they had wings. They were a bit more slender and graceful than a T-Rex though.

Alanna scuttled away in panic when Rannathor came with heavy thumping awkward steps closer to her. The girl dragon's eyes and thick eyelashes batted at her.

"What do you want?" she huffed her question.

Rannathor did not answer and appeared to be bobbing her head up and down.

"She wants to get to know you ..." Lady Eilin came and kneeled next to Alanna.

"I-I ... I don't know ... I'm not sure ..."

"It is alright. The dragons and you will need time with one another."

Rannathor understood Eilin's words. She nodded gently and moved back to where the other dragons were still standing.

That was a gentle gesture that Alanna appreciated so much. She stood up, and caught a glance of Tristan. She remembered what she had just heard: Anthor, the oldest and the tallest dragon, was the king's ride. Tristan was the king and a dragon rider. There was the royal family who was the dragons' guardian and rider, and there was House of Evara, her ancestral family, who was the healer. She repeated those in her head like she was studying for an upcoming exam—it felt like that to her, that she had to learn so many new stuff, stuff that she did not even know how to begin to convince herself that they were real and believable.

The king who had been standing in silence a few steps behind Lady Eilin now looked straight at Alanna though Alanna could not really decipher what he felt or thought at that moment. But those captivating blue eyes searched her and Alanna found herself entangled in the gaze.

"She is a bad omen! Do not let her get close our king!" all of a sudden someone shouted from behind Alanna, and that brought her back to the moment here.

She turned around, and saw a man in his fifties, short and burly with grey eyes and bald head, came running while lifting his fist up. He ran toward her and the anger in his eyes made Alanna take a few steps back.

"How come she is here? Lady Eilin! You are endangering Alathyr even further by bringing your daughter back!" the man screamed, Tristan blocked him from charging to Alanna.

"The dragons called her! It is time for her to be back here, in her own land, with her own people! She is my daughter and not a bad omen!" Lady Eilin screamed back.

"Carrus! Stop!" Tristan pushed the man he called Carrus back a bit.

"Your Majesty, she is bad news for Alathyr! She was born out of forbidden love, out of Pan's grace!" Carrus paused to take a breath and continued,"It is a well-kept secret but we know it, we know about Lady Eilin and her secret child. You do know that too, Your Majesty!"

Tristan thought for a moment before replying to Carrus,"She survived the trip across the tunnel and the door of Pan. Pan would never anyone with bad intentions to pass through safely. She means no harm to Alathyr!"

Lady Eilin nodded her head hard and spoke with obvious fury in her shaking voice, "My daughter has paid enough for my foolishness. She stays here with her family. Carrus, I will guard her, and nothing you can do to harm her!"

Carrus groaned in anger and bellowed, "I am the advisor to the king! My words should mean something here!"

Alanna froze, her body felt cold and stiff. She was embarrassed, yes. Angry, yes. Scared, yes. She tried hard to wrap her mind around the fact that she had been uprooted from a world she had known so well, a world where she had all her plans set, a world she had to leave behind because those dragons who stood in front of her wanted to meet her here.

Now this. A public scourge of who she was because apparently her birth mother's rebellious, scandalous love affair in the past that resulted in her birth was not a secret anymore, at least not to these high-ranking individuals in Alathyr.

"Let us all go back to the main hall," the king spoke, though it was clear he spoke directly to his advisor, the hysterical Carrus.

Carrus shot an angry glance at Alanna.

"Carrus, it is an order! We go back up!" Tristan walked closer to Carrus and stared at the burly man with fiery focus and power. Carrus nodded to his king, shot an angry glance at Alanna before finally turning and following Tristan who had gone first.

Alanna stood still. She was not sure what she was thinking about actually. She was just shocked. Shocked and afraid and confused.

"Alanna?" it was Mom's, her adoptive Mom, voice followed by a gentle tap on her shoulder. "Let's go up again."

Alanna shook her head. She did not wish to see Carrus again, not right now. The dragons suddenly felt so much friendlier than Carrus, a human.

"I will stay with her down here with the dragons," Lady Eilin nodded at Dad and Mom. The two nodded back at their lady and walked away after a couple worried glance back at Alanna.

There she was. Standing facing the dragons who seemed to be intently studying her. Their eyes widened, their breathing slow, and they just stared at her in a way that weirdly calming for her.

And Lady Eilin stood a few steps next to her. Her actual mom.

"I am so confused ... so scared ..." she finally said what she had always wanted to say from the time she got here.

"I am so sorry that things happen this way for you, dear Alanna."

"I don't need apology. I just want to go back to my life ... my old-old life."

Lady Eilin was quiet with heavy sigh that marked her worry. "Something about you resonate with the dragons. They want you close, they call you. Being farther away from them will make them call louder to you, and ..."

"The headaches ..."

"Yes."

"Am I a dragon healer? Like you?"

Lady Eilin now turned to Alanna. She smiled. "Would you like to be?"

"No-no I don't think that'll work. I have plans with my life, you see. I am a dog walker. Not a dragon healer. I also want to study further. I want to ... do research ... I want to build a dogwalking company. I-I have plans."

Lady Eilin let out a gentle chuckle. Alanna turned and her eyes met her mother's. Those eyes shone with gentleness and a certain mischief. "Well, the dragons are not your common beasts, Alanna. They are the companions of Pan, they are the ride of the gods when they go to battles against the underworld. Our king rode Anthor in wars to protect Alathyr. These dragons have their will, their wishes."

"So? Am I just supposed to put my life on hold, cancel all plans, just for them?"

Lady Eilin sighed and her gentle face turned gloomy. "Yes. That is the ... curse ... for lack of better word, of being in the House of Evara. If you are chosen by the dragons, they become your life, your future. You cannot even choose to whom you will give your heart and love to."

Alanna closed her eyes. Bragan, a father she would never meet. Bragan and Eilin, young and in love, and all was crushed by the weight of Eilin's lifelong duty and destiny.

But something else caught her attention.

"What has happened, Lady Eilin? Why are you and the king down here ...?" she asked. No, she could not call the woman in front of her as Mom. Not yet at least.

Lady Eilin bit her lips and shivered as she answered Alanna, "You have an aunt. My twin sister. Thyrra. She caused all these madness."

Chapter 8

Thyrra was born a few minutes earlier than Eilin. The twin sisters were close as one would expect twins would be. They were different in terms of personality though. Thyrra was studious, quiet, serious, ambitious, and did everything excellently. While Eilin was carefree, stubborn, with infectious laugh and a rebel-at-heart. Thyrra had always had Eilin's back, even when Eilin got herself into a lot of trouble with their strict parents.

However their closeness started to crack when Eilin, when she was 18, was chosen by the dragons to be the dragon healer.

Ambitious Thyrra who had worked hard to win affection of the dragons found it unfair. She felt that she was the one who had studied, who had taken her role seriously as a member of House of Evara, and she was the one who was supposed to be chosen, not her stubborn and rebellious younger sister Eilin.

Eilin tried to make sure Thyrra know how much she meant to her and would go to Thyrra frequently for advice as she prepared herself to be a dragon healer.

But along came Bragan.

It was Bragan that broke all the connection between the sisters.

Thyrra fell in love with Bragan, but Bragan had always loved Eilin, and Eilin loved Bragan.

When Eilin eloped with Bragan, Thyrra turned raging mad. She was beyond furious. She could never forgive Eilin—Eilin was the dragon healer, a role she had so coveted and desired, and now Eilin snatched away the only man she had ever loved, Bragan. Thyrra felt betrayed and destroyed by her own twin sister.

In her dark rage, she vowed she would destroy Eilin, thus she secretly surrendered herself to be a servant of Erebus, the dark demon god of the underworld.

Erebus started changing Thyrra by teaching her dark sorcery.

Thyrra stayed quiet in the shadow as Eilin's life with Bragan unfolded and destroyed. She also stayed quiet when Alanna was taken away, and the world passed her by as she hid herself in a tower of rocks in a forest far away from her home. Erebus made sure she was isolated, and the darkness within Thyrra grew stronger and stronger as years went by.

Thyrra never spoke to anyone, did not want to have contact with anyone, especially with Eilin who she would always see as her enemy, the destroyer of her life and dreams.

A few months ago, Thyrra, with help from the dark forces of Erebus, finally became strong enough to stage a shocking coup of the throne. It was shocking because she had stayed so quiet behind the shadow that noone really thought of her anymore.

Her dark power had grown to be so great that it could prolong winter and make it colder than normal. Erebus' forces, legions of snake-faced human-bodied monsters sprung up from the deep abyss and war broke between the forces of Alathyr and the forces of Thyrra and Erebus.

A bloody battle flared for days, the dragons fought for Alathyr, and King Tristan rode Anthor to fight the winged demons that were also sent by Erebus. However, Alathyr forces had to admit defeat when fatalities mounted among civilians, and the dragons were wounded.

King Tristan decided to ask the dragons to bring them all, the palace officials, the soldiers, and the civilians that they could gather to the enchanted dragons' lair.

The dragons flew in front of them, and the King and the rest would follow them. The enemy forces who had tried to chase them would be lost in the forest and died because they could not get out.

It was then that the human beings realized that Knyra—the waterfall that people of Alathyr knew existed but noone knew where it was—was actually the gate to the dragons' lair.

Strangely, after they got into the massive catacombs like structure, the memory of how to get to the dragons' lair could only be remembered by the king, Tristan. The dragons through their telepathy had ensured that the secred hideout was only known and be traced by one person, the reigning king of Alathyr. That was why the king, who now led a band of rebels to try to always shake Alathyr's defense, had to always lead his soldiers out in the world above the catacombs. Only he knew how to bring them all back to the dragons' lair again.

Thyrra became Queen Thyrra now, and the demon forces of Erebus strengthened her armies. Her revenge was not done though. She wanted the dragons dead, Eilin dead, and the king dead.

The wounded dragons started their healing with Lady Eilin. Though they were not completely healed yet.

"That's ... crazy..." Alanna struggled to contain all the events in her head. To top it all off, she had an evil family member. Aunt Thyrra. The one whose evil rage had caused a prolonged winter and a destruction to the normal living at Alathyr.

Eilin coughed hard, her back heaved up and down as she coughed. When she finished coughing, there was a fresh droplet of blood at the corner of her lips.

"Lady Eilin ... you are injured," Alanna rushed closer to the woman, her mother.

"I am weakened because I have spent most of my energy trying to heal the dragons. Maybe they know this and that was why they called out to you. They want to see if they can trust you to be a healer."

Alanna turned to look at the dragons, all four now laid on the rocky floor.

"They are telepathic, Alanna. They feel the healer. They speak to me through their mind."

"How do I know if they trust me enough to be their healer?"

"They will bow to you and you will hear them speak in your mind. They will vow their trust to you."

"I heard murmurs before in my head, when I had my headache."

"The dragons are worried about the state of Alathyr now with Queen Thyrra, and about my own declining health," Lady Eilin coughed again.

Alanna nodded though she was not sure she completely understood what had happened so far in her life.

After spending a few minutes in silence there with the dragons, Alanna and Lady Eilin went up again to the main hall. Mom and Dad had gotten a place for them to spend the night, a small rock room in one of the corridors. Mom and Dad were then busy going around and managed to find some old friends of theirs that after some tearful reunions, they helped her find some clothes for them and Alanna too.

One middle-aged woman, a childhood friend of Mom, came to see Alanna. She was a frail-looking woman who wore thick jackets and wide skirt.

"We have heard all about you, sweet girl. It is alright. No bad omen here. If our king trusts you, we trust you!" she said while patting Alanna's shoulder. Suddenly she went around and watched Alanna's figure closely. "You have good waist! You will bear many healthy babies!"

Alanna almost choked on her own breath she heard that while Mom whisked her friend away. "That was appropriate," Alanna huffed in annoyance.

It took some getting used to for Alanna to live in such underground commune. First of all, she did not know what time it was, or what day it was outside. After a few hours of going with Dad and Mom to learn stuff about the commune, Alanna guessed it must have been late night because she did feel sleepy now. Mom and Dad went to sleep while Alanna decided she still wanted to sit outside by the communal fireplace.

As her eyes watched the flames danced on the fireplace, Lady Eilin dropped by and said goodnight to her. They talked for a bit, it was mostly Alanna answering her questions about her life in her other universe. And that became awkward to her.

"Look, Lady Eilin. I know you are trying to-to connect with me. I want to do that too. I hope you understand that this has been so-so crazy. I hope you understand ... I am sorry ..." she hoped she did not offend her, she was just still reeling from all that had happened to her.

Lady Eilin smiled. "I understand. I, along with the dragons, will give you space." She nodded and bid her goodnight once more and went downstairs, she had her room close to the dragons.

The massive hall became quieter now, the inhabitants had gone back to their rooms carved out of massive rocks.

According to what she had heard from Mom who had heard it from her friends here, this place was build thousands of years ago when the dragons were younger and Pan had helped the building of this catacombs, this underground structure. Early Alathyrians had built this for the dragons, and Pan's magic turned it enchanted to become a safe haven for the dragons and Alathyrians in times of darkness like this.

People who lived in here had to hunt and gather food from the forest and rivers around here. The king—the only one who knew how to get back to the catacombs—would lead the search for food and water once a week, they would then bring the sustenance back and cured the meat, made jams from the fruits, and stored water in large clay buckets.

Only about a hundred or so Alathyrians who lived here now, thus each and every one of them had multiple family members who still lived in fear under the oppression of Queen Thyrra's rule. It was tragic, and it had been what motivated the king to lead a band of his best warriors on the lookout in forests and villages around here. They would kidnap Alathyrians and bring them here to the catacombs, as well as killing as many Thyrra's forces as they could. Now Thyrra's forces consisted of two legions: The human legions were the former Alathyr soldiers of all ranks who decided to surrender and give their allegiance to the new ruler, out of fear or promises of gold and glory. The second, more dangerous legions, were the snake-faced human-bodied soldiers of Erebus.

Alanna was startled from her mind wandering when she heard footsteps coming from behind her. Tippy-tappy of feet on the quiet cavernous hall became loud enough to catch her attention.

She turned around and could not help but smile.

A dog, a white siberian husky stood a few meters behind her with tail wagging and tongue hanging. The husky was large, had striking light blue eyes, and a long bushy tail.

"Hey you ... come here, sweetie!" she turned completely to face the husky and extended her right hand. She felt much lighter upon seeing the dog. She had missed her beastie besties so much.

The dog let out a gentle growl and walked toward her. Then she saw it clearly. The dog walked with a limp because it only had three legs. The front right leg was missing.

The husky got to her and started licking her face while she rubbed the ears. She laughed, and was surprised to hear herself laughing again.

"Be careful with Filip. He will steal your heart and whatever crumble of food you have," Alanna looked up to see who was talking to her.

It was Tristan.

Alanna stopped rubbing the dog's ears, and nodded. "They are experts in those."

Tristan took a deep breath and walked closer to her, then he sat in front of her.

Filip went to his human and started rubbing his head on Tristan's chest.

Alanna felt like all words had left her mind when she stared at Tristan's eyes. The dark blue eyes seemed to shine in the warm glow of the fireplace.

"Thank you ... for saving me today from the giant crows," she found her words.

Tristan just gave a faint nod. "I guess you have heard about what happened in this land. Those giant crows are just one among many wretched happenings here."

"You are a king," Alanna was not sure why she said that. She had read about the lives of kings and queens and all their royal dalliances, but to meet an actual king in front of her, was still something strange for her.

"A king who had lost his throne," Tristan stared at her unblinked. "I have no throne. No honor."

Filip barked as if he disagreed with his human.

"I guess you are lucky to still have Filip," Alanna was not sure that was the thing to say, but she was a dog person, and Tristan seemed like he was one too.

"An old gentleman this. Fifteen years. He has been my friend since I was a child."

"Three legs?"

"I fell in a river shortly after I got him. He jumped into the river to pull me to safety, and his leg was bitten by a water snake. Poisonous. He lost his leg that day."

Alanna nodded, and Filip laid on the floor next to Tristan now, his eyes closed and his snoring sound was loud enough to be heard.

"And ... Alanna, do stay away from my advisor Carrus."

"He hates me."

"Some people here still think you bring bad luck to this land."

"How about you?"

"I believe our beloved god Pan will not let any more calamity fall on this land by letting a bad omen pass by his door safely."

Alanna sighed a relief breath. "Good. At least you would not have me executed."

"Why would I have you executed?"

"Isn't that what a king do to-to troublesome people?"

"I would have let you die by the claws of the crows if I want to do away with you."

Alanna was quiet. Tristan could have let her perish without even touching her. That was indeed true.

Tristan nodded one time at her, got up, and left. Filip woke up and followed his human.

Alanna decided to just sit there. Tristan had earned a place in the deepest crevice of her mind, a place she had kept for herself and her most private thoughts.

Chapter 9

Alanna did not even sleep much at all that night. She could not hear bird chirping or sun caressing her face in the morning, and she got up when she saw everyone else had started their activities.

She walked around, exhausted and zombie-like, trying to ask if Mom and Dad needed help with anything. They were busy trying to set up their own family kitchen and food supplies. She helped a bit with that, then she was just wandering mindlessly.

Carrus saw her, and his eyes followed her moves like a hawk following a prey. She ignored him, she remembered what Tristan had told her, to stay away from Carrus and that was what she would do. She did nothing wrong. All she wanted now was get out of this underground settlement. She wanted to see the snow again. The sun. The trees. Fresh air. All. Outside.

Then Filip came to her. She smiled and kneeled to pet him. Filip knew she was sad, a dog would understand and feel the vibe around a human. He buried his head within Alanna's embrace and that calmed Alanna down.

Two young children, about four or five years old, came running to her and asked her questions. She smiled and was happy to answer them—questions about her name, what she was doing, did she like Filip. What a breath of fresh air!

The children started rubbing Filip's belly when someone shouted from behind them. "Aran! Dilla! Come!"

The two children startled and turned around. A plump woman in her thirties were waving at them. She did look cross.

"Do not play with that stranger! She could be bad luck!" the woman screamed again, waving her hand more aggressively toward Aran and Dilla, most likely her children.

The two children turned and stared at Alanna now with a renewed fear like they were staring at a human who had just transformed herself to be a flesh-eating, children-snatching monster. Their eyes widened, and the two stood up and rushed back to their mother.

Alanna was shocked, and she did feel pangs of hurt in her heart. The woman took her children and shot a nasty glance at Alanna.

"I am not-not a bad omen, or bad luck … that's not fair," she stammered her own defense toward the woman, but the woman did not even look at her anymore because she was now busy reprimanding her two young children. Some passersby slowed their steps to watch what was happening, and that added to Alanna's embarrassment because they too were looking at her with such disgust and fear.

Carrus, that mean advisor, it must have been him who had spread fear about her among the people here. Alanna covered her mouth with her palms, trying to stifle the coming sob, then she shook her head at Filip. Filip's blue eyes trained on her, and she started sobbing quietly. Filip was quiet, and snuggled his snout on Alanna's lap.

Time just passed by as she sat on the floor with Filip resting his head on her lap. The dog was old and calm, that was for sure. She had two huskies in her dogwalking roster, and none of them was even close in calmness to Filip.

Mom and Dad came to check on her, and she was thankful that her tears had dried up by then. They brought her bread and simple soup, all they could find in the underground commune's supply of ingredients for cooking. She feigned interest in eating, and that made them happy. She could see creases of worry deepened on their face, though they tried to look lighthearted in front of her.

"Are you alright?" Dad patted her hand.

"Yes-yes ... I am. I-just-I just need to get used to the life here."

"Lady Eilin is still with the dragons downstairs. You can go see her," Mom volunteered an idea.

She nodded. Mom and Dad looked at each other and smiled. Mom said, "We are going to be busy taking care some things here. We are living here for now, there are things to move, things to collect ..."

"Don't worry about me, Mom, Dad. I will be fine. Oh, this is Filip! Tristan's dog."

"His Majesty, Alanna. Not just Tristan," Dad corrected her.

She nodded, not sure she could stick to calling Tristan His Majesty. It would be too weird.

"Beautiful dog ..." Mom patted Filip's head.

Dad gave her a quick peck on the top of her head before he and Mom left to try to set up a life for their family here. Am I still part of their family? Or am I a part of House of Evara now? Can one be fully part of two families? She wondered. Unraveled. That was what she felt. Like a tight-knit wool that was sliced and now all the intertwined threads fell apart, unraveled. Lost.

Filip stretched his body and sauntered away, the moment Alanna decided that she would just go and visit the dragons and Lady Eilin. She walked slowly, her eyes darted here and there, maybe she wanted to find Tristan but he was nowhere to be seen.

She kept walking and gingerly went down the long winding rock staircase to go to the dragons downstairs. As she went down the stairs, the faces of the children she had met earlier and the fear in their eyes haunted her again. I am not a monster, she repeated to herself. But still, she knew that, but to think that she had scared some kids because of who she was made her felt pretty awful.

When she got to the dragons' hall, Lady Eilin was kneeling on the ground. Her arms pushed down to support her, and she breathed heavy.

"Alanna ..." she turned and called out to her.

Lady Eilin's face was pale, and Alanna rushed and kneeled next to her. "Are you alright? You look pale," she reached for Lady Eilin's hand and rubbed it. It was cold. Eilin coughed hard and a drop of blood was at the corner of her lips again.

"Alanna, good to see you down here again," Lady Eilin caressed Alanna's cheek. Her eyes widened and she smiled,"I can see your father's eyes in you. You have your father's eyes. Oh Bragan would have loved you so much," Eilin almost cried when she touched Alanna's eyes gently with her trembling fingertips.

Bragan. A father she would never know. Alanna sighed and massaged Lady Eilin's hand within the clasp of her hand. "How was he? Bragan, my-my father ..."

Eilin looked at her, smiling ear to ear upon hearing Alanna addressing Bragan as her father. The dragon healer was rejuvenated and started talking,"Bragan, your father, was a kind, handsome man. He had a way with all kinds of animals. Animals just loved him. He was quiet, thoughtful, and he hated his job as a mansion guard. He had to do it because he was an orphan, and his foster family was poor and he needed the income to help them."

Alanna nodded. Her curiosity was piqued about Bragan, her biological father.

They were quiet for some time and the dragons were also quiet, it was like they understood that the two needed a moment together.

Alanna thought before speaking again,"I don't know if I would like it to be a dragon healer, Lady Eilin. I have my plans, my life, in the universe across from the door of Pan."

Eilin shook her head."I do not know what I can do to help you with that, dear Alanna. The dragons will show if they trust you enough, and if they do, they will keep chasing you to do your duty. I-I wish I could help you, Alanna."

"I want to be the one who determines my own life, my own destiny. Not the dragons."

"I understand, Alanna. I eloped with your father as a way to choose my own destiny. But you see how it ended. It ended with such tragedy for you, for me, and for him."

One of the dragons purred loud enough for the two of them to turn to see which one it was that purred. It was Rannathor, the girl dragon. She lifted her head and her large eyes trained upon Alanna. Rannathor's breath suddenly became faster, and she turned toward Anthor, the oldest dragon. Drathor and Selivor were also staring at Anthor with full focus.

"What is happening?"

Lady Eilin did not answer, her eyes closed and she shook. Sweats broke on her forehead, and she trembled. She opened her eyes again, and this time the oldest dragon Anthor stood still and stared straight at Eilin.

Eilin maintained an eye contact with Anthor, and started shivering like she was cold. "Anthor spoke to me through his mind. He said ..." Lady Eilin shook her head.

"Said what?" Alanna could not help but feeling an ominous sense of something horrible descending upon her.

Lady Eilin started weeping, turned to Alanna. "Alanna ... oh no ..." she muttered, then she lunged to Alanna and hugged her tight.

"Lady Eilin, what's going on?"

"Anthor told me his prophecy. The king, Alanna ... the king's fate. His majesty's rise or fall. It will depend on you."

Lady Eilin hugged her tighter and wept in breathless sobs.

Alanna froze, she could smell faint fragrance of flowers in her birth mother's hair, she could feel the wetness of her tears on her cheek. But her brain struggled to process what her mother had just told her. Her arms hugged Lady Eilin back, awkward and confused.

Tristan's fate depended on her. What did that even suppose to mean? She was just a bad omen, a stranger brought here to Alathyr, and he was the king of the land. What could she do to cause his rise or fall?

Lady Eilin stopped crying and released her hug from around Alanna.

"Only Anthor has the gift of prophecy and he rarely speaks of it to me, to a human. But he did, just now. Oh Alanna, I am very worried about you."

"Lady Eilin, I am now more worried about my future plans if the dragons choose me to be their healer. I am sorry but I really don't know what to say about a dragon's prophecy ..." Alanna whispered to Eilin.

Eilin bit her lips and nodded with a thin smile. "I will pray to the gods for you, for your safety, my daughter."

Alanna nodded. "That'll be very kind of you," she smiled back.

But Lady Eilin was bothered, and Alanna knew Anthor's telepathy to her birth mother just now was strong enough to shake her.

She stayed with Lady Eilin for a while, watching her give the dragons massages, patting them, whispering to their ears, preparing a big bowl of herbs then cleaning their wounds—the wounds from the battle with Erebus' forces some months ago—with it.

But the vibe had changed. Lady Eilin was sad, that much was clear. Worry creases deepened on her forehead and wore down her mischievous stare. The dragons were quiet too.

When she was going to go to the upper floor again, Lady Eilin asked her not to tell anyone about Anthor's prophecy. "A dragon's prophecy is sensitive, Alanna. We do not know what is going to happen if you tell this to anyone, so please do not tell especially not to His Majesty. A dragon's prophecy about his life may end up ruining him and his bond with the dragon if he knows. And ... some people here will jump at any chance to drive you away. Let's not add more reasons for them to think of you as bad luck."

To that Alanna agreed.

Chapter 10

The rest of the day Alanna was just walking around to the different levels of the catacomb-like structure. Some people watched her with curiosity in their eyes, and to these people she tried to smile—these were the ones with some potential for her to have a more amicable interaction. Some others turned their back as soon they they saw her, or watched her with furrowed brows and suspicious glance. These were the ones she just avoided eye contact altogether and walked away as quiet as she could.

Mom and Dad had set up their little cubicle-like family settlement, a far cry from their apartment in Oakridge, but it would do for now at least.

What amused Alanna was to see her parents' reaction to the simple food, drink, little things here and there that they had missed so much during their time in Oakridge. Their hushed squeals, the excitement in their eyes, all made Alanna feel that maybe it was fine to come here. Though in a strange way, she felt that she understood what it felt like for her parents to just be uprooted from their home on a moment's notice and left without knowing when they could come back to Alathyr, their homeland. She was in the exact same predicament as they had been years ago. They came back here finally, so maybe she could go back to Oakridge somehow someday, without the torturous headaches and maddening murmuring of the dragons.

A childhood friend of Dad came to visit, and he looked somewhat uncomfortable with Alanna there, so Alanna came up with a reason (she wanted to visit the dragons) to leave her family cubicle.

She walked away, and she missed the outside world so much. She needed to know what time it was now. She had been trying to keep track within herself the possible time by noticing how tired she was.

She had spent hours today with Lady Eilin, and hours with her parents. They had some sort of plain bread and watery soup dinner again, then they spoke for hours, before the friend of Dad stopped by. So it should be quite late at night now.

As she sat by the common fireplace, the prophecy of Anthor entered her mind again. Tristan's fate depended on her. What does that mean?What could she do to cause such great influence on a king's life, a king and a dragon rider none less? She wondered while her eyes watched the dance of the flames in fronf of her.

And Tristan had been on her mind a lot. There was a gnawing worry that crept within her heart; would she be a big trouble for Tristan? Would he be hurt because of her? That could not be. She would not want to be the cause of pain for him.

A gentle poke on her waist interrupted her wandering mind. She turned to see the cause of the poke, startled, and smiled.

Filip had come to her, and in her busy mind, she had not noticed it until the old three-legged husky pushed his snout gently onto her waist.

"Hey! What's up, old man!" she ruffled Filip's fur, scratched him behind his ear, and Filip plopped himself on the ground with his belly up. Expecting more ear scratches and belly rubs. Alanna laughed and gave Filip some vigorous belly rubs.

"Thank you for being my friend here, sweet Filip," she whispered to Filip. Filip's blue eyes watched her, one of his ears twitched, head tilted, and he got up.

"Well, now go. Tristan must be waiting for you," she patted Filip's head.

Filip stayed still, did a big stretch, and sat up with his eyes glued on her.

"Go! Go, sweet Filip!" she smiled and waved her hand to tell Filip to go. "Find Tristan!"

Filip moved closer to her as if it was one of those do-the-opposite day, which she knew was quite common among her dog clients.

Then the dog tippy-tappy walked closer to her again, and grabbed her hand with his mouth.

"Filip? What?"

Filip kept pulling her and she decided to stand up and follow the husky.

The dog let go of her hand and limped with his three legs slightly ahead of her, turning his head often to make sure she was still following behind.

Alanna followed Filip into one of the corridors, and kept walking in the narrow passageway with rock rooms to her left and right. The dim light of the few torches made her watch her steps especially carefully. They got to the end of the corridor, and made a right turn to another corridor with much less rooms. It looked like a labyrinth here with all the turns and rooms. Though Filip walked in full confidence, showing that this whole place was his playground.

They got to the end of this corridor, and it was a dead end with one room at the left side.

Alanna entered the room and was in awe.

There were books, piles of books carefully placed against the rock wall. There was also a wooden table, massive oak table with all kinds of carving tools there: Carving knives, mallets, chisels. A log of an oak tree, halved to form a half circle the size of Alanna's arm, was on the table with some carving started to form on it. A work not yet finished.

"Filip? Why did you bring me here?" her eyes busy scanned the whole table, Filip stood next to her, tail wagging and tongue hanging low.

"What are you doing here?" Alanna let out a shriek then turned around to find the source of the voice.

Tristan stood at the entrance. Filip barked one time and ran charging with its happy tail wagging at his human.

"I am sorry I don't mean to come to your-your place here without your permission. Filip brought me here. Are the books ... the carving tools ... yours?"

Tristan recovered from his surprise and nodded. "All mine. Whatever left of my previous life as a king." He sighed, patted Filip's head, and turned to Alanna again. "I am sorry if Filip has dragged you here and taken it upon himself to show you this room. He has never done it before. I guess he likes you."

Alanna could not contain a smile on her face. "Dogs would bring little gifts to the human they like. I guess Filip just brings me your room."

Filip turned and now ran to her, tail still wagging.

"I-I will just take my leave now."

"Do stay. I do not mind."

"Carrus would go berserk if he finds out that I am here."

"Do not mind him."

"Why?"

Tristan looked confused, he tilted his head so that the black claw tattoo on the side of his head looked like it moved, and his captivating blue eyes conveyed his what do you mean why? in such a perfect wordless message.

"Why are you so-so calm about me? You could just order me to be executed, or to be left out there to be eaten by those-those gigantic crows."

"What is it with you and execution?"

"Well, kings do those stuff, right? If they don't like someone?"

"What makes you think I do not like you?"

"Well, hello? Bad omen?"

"I believe in Pan and his wise judgment. He let you pass through his door. You do not have any ill intention toward Alathyr. Evil Thyrra will never be able to pass through that door. That is what protecting your world on the other side, Alanna." Tristan walked closer, and the room felt like it was contracting smaller. "Thyrra wants me dead though to before that she has to find a way to get here, to get to this enchanted dragon's lair. Erebus wants the dragon destroyed so they cannot fight against him and his darkness ever again. Thyrra wants the dragons dead so she could absorb their magic and be stronger, and maybe pass through the Pan's door if she is strong enough. I have darker things to worry about than about you being a bad omen, Alanna. This land is in a prolonged winter now, and it is already in its darkest moment even without you coming here."

Alanna could see the practical logic behind that statement. Alathyr was already in big trouble even before she set foot here. That was the fact.

From the corner of her eyes, she could see Filip laying with ease on the entrance. She could have sworn Filip had that contented look on its face, like it had planned to take her here, it worked, and he could relax now.

Tristan's tall body-he was at least a head taller than her, solid and ripped, stood two arm-lengths from her, and she felt a strange sense of contradiction: of coldness and warmth, of fear and calmnness. Her heart thumped hard and words dissipated from her mind. She had wanted to say something, anything, but now, standing there in front of him, she could not find the words. Her lips trembled and she shook her head gently. She figured out what to say. "You are-quite a reader ... and wood carving. I never thought ..."

"Just because I am good with arrows you didn't think I could read?" Tristan took another step closer, and she took one step back.

"That's not what I meant, Tristan. I-I hope it is alright if I call you Tristan. I am not yet used to calling someone Your Majesty."

"Tristan is fine. I read a lot, Alanna. I carve wood. Reading books and carving wood and Filip help me keep my sanity."

Alanna nodded. "May I see your books?"

Tristan took a few steps back and extended his right arm to the books, telling Alanna in gesture that she may have a look at his books.

Alanna went and kneeled by the first out of five or six piles of books. She took one book, old and bound by some sort of animal skin, and started flipping the pages.

She did not understand some of the texts because it was written in what could be Alathyrians' ancient language. But from the images drawn with charcoal, she could guess what the book was about. Medicine.

Then another book, and this one she had no idea what it was.

She turned and looked at Tristan. "What is this one about?"

"Battle strategies. Written by my great grandfather in ancient Alathyrian language."

Alanna nodded, and took another book. This one was a small, pocket-sized even. Bound by red-dyed animal skin, adorned with a stalk of dried grass, and when she opened it, she smiled when she saw the drawings.

"I would venture to guess this one is a recipe book? Tristan? You cook too?"

And he sheepishly smiled, and that smile stopped Alanna's heartbeat for a moment. Shy and handsome smile. "No, Alanna. I am clueless in the kitchen. It was my mother's. Before my father passed away, she spent a lot of time doing what she liked best. Cooking. She wrote them all down with drawings of the ingredients too. After my father passed, she had to take the throne as a regent, a caretaker of the throne until I became old enough to ascend the throne." Tristan turned gloomy, and he continued,"She became someone else after she took the throne. She was not a warm mother anymore. She never cooked anymore. Or played with me. Her waking hours were spent worrying about the throne. She had passed away now, but for me it felt like she had been gone for much longer than her death."

Alanna bit her lips, shook her head when she realized the sad reality of being so close to the throne."I don't know, Tristan. I just lived my life as a regular girl in my other world. I don't know anything about the throne, the intrigues around it. But if it meant you lost your mother to it, then I don't think I want to be anywhere near it."

"Good for you."

Alanna turned to Tristan, and Tristan just stared at her with such curiosity, such gentle gaze that she felt comfortable enough now to speak more. "I don't want to be here. To be a dragon healer. I hope they don't choose me—the dragons. I have dreams in my other world, Tristan."

"My dream was to carve wood for living. That was all. I could make really good carvings that could fetch good selling price. I hated my life as a crown prince, I never had any time for anything fun."

Alanna smiled. "Here we are. Two people with crushed dreams at the foot of the throne and the service of the dragons."

Tristan paused, then he looked at Alanna with curiosity. "What are your dreams?"

Alanna took a deep breath, chuckled, and started explaining in simple terms what her dreams were: Going to grad school to study psychology, and building her own dogwalking small business. She spent quite a bit of time giving descriptions of her beastie besties, her dog clients—how they looked like, how they behaved, funny quirks they had.

It took some explanation for Tristan to understand what psychology and graduate school were, but his eyes shone with contentment when he finally grasped the gist of it. Though dogwalking was something that still intrigued him.

"You walk dogs and people pay you?"

"Yes indeed."

"Interesting."

Alanna was quiet for a bit, Tristan sat next to her on the floor among the piles of books. "I just hope I will survive whatever that's going to happen to me here. I don't want to die, Tristan," she tried talking with as much strength as she could muster, but her voice broke and the shiver was obvious. She was damn afraid, that was for sure.

"You will survive. I will do whatever it takes so you can be safe here. I promise, Alanna."

Chapter 11

She spent some time with Tristan, after browsing his carvings—which showed the immense talent that he had in this craft, they just sat next to each other in silence. The room seemed big enough for them to have their own thought wander, at the same time it felt small enough for them to sit with their arms touched each other, albeit they moved closer without even realizing it.

The strangeness of meeting, talking, sitting next to a king of such a faraway land had dissipated for Alanna. Tristant just seemed so normal for her, a guy with dreams, a guy who could not get away with and simply had to do what he had been tasked to do, to fulfill his destiny as a king who not only was a skilled archer but also a talented woodcarver and an avid reader.

Tristan had depth that her heart, the untamed version of it, wanted to delve into wholeheartedly. But her logical mind analyzed the whole situation and told her to keep her distance and leave it that way. You don't want to get hurt again now, do you? Remember who he is and who you are. Keep your distance. That was what her brain told her to.

So that was it. Her logical brain won.

She bid her goodnight after that, and Tristan just nodded. When she went back to her cubicle, her parents were not asleep yet and they told her they had started to worry about her. Life had changed so much for her, but at least this part remained: Her parents, adoptive parents, who would stay up no matter how late it was to wait for her to come home. That felt good as her life began here at its earnest.

The next few days for her was a progression of the increasing feeling of familiarity to the place. She started to get to know the different alleyways of the underground settlement, and she took some mental notes of people to avoid and people to smile at. Nobody really spoke to her. Not yet at least.

Carrus hated her, he would glare at her whenever she caught his gaze. But she took Tristan's advice: Do not mind him. Laying low and be inconspicuous may be her best bet at surviving here.

Lady Eilin was still coughing a lot and her complexion grew more pale. Mom spent more time downstairs with her and the dragons, and Alanna would be there too. She promised herself to try to build a bridge to connect with her biological mom, and Lady Eilin reciprocated. She told Alanna little things about the dragons. The quiet and pensive Anthor, the obstinate but gentle Selivor, the always curious Drathor—he would lay and rest his large head next to Lady Eilin so she could read for him, and the sweet and carefree Rannathor, the one girl who always got protected by her brothers.

It was her budding friendship with Tristan that somehow worried her a bit. Tristan became closer to her, he would visit her at random times whenever he got a break, and Carrus did not find that amusing. Alanna did not want Tristan to get in trouble. Carrus hated her more, she knew for sure.

Tristan gave her permission to be at his library, so at night she would read at Tristan's makeshift library, although she had to choose the books without ancient characters. She had enjoyed her quiet time among the books. She did not bring her own books of course. Books were the last thing on her mind when she was whisked away to Alathyr with life-threatening headache and maddening murmurs of the dragons. Tristan would not be there usually, he was still busy with whatever he had to do. But Filip was there, just laying next to her.

She realized that it may be a life that she had to get used to, whether she liked it or not. Tristan showed he cared about her: He quietly watched over her, made sure Carrus stay away from her and her family, and stood up for her when Carrus made a fuss about anything she did or did not do.

She dared not venture to even predict where her friendship with Tristan would go, she had enough heartache with Jake to last her a lifetime. And to date a king, with his angry advisor and his additional duty as the leader of a band of warriors who tried to shake a kingdom, with the dragons and their wishes at the background? That seemed like a recipe for a heartbreak, and she had enough of that.

And the premonition of Anthor: Tristan's rise or fall would depend on her. That still scared her, bothered her a lot, though she had decided that she would keep it to herself. Only Lady Eilin knew about it besides her. That was enough.

She knew the dragon healer had been praying for her, for Tristan, and for Alathyr.

She hoped prayers to the gods would be enough to avert whatever bad luck that was coming her way.

That night, though it had grown late, she was still reading a book on Alathyr's geography in Tristan's library, a book she chose because she was intrigued by the drawings of the various regions done in different naturally-sourced dye colours.

Once in a while she would pause her reading and just stare to the rock ceiling. She counted in her head, and she was pretty sure she had been down here in this settlement for about a week. A week of not going to her dogwalking responsibilities. She had lost all her clients by now. She was sure of that, that and she must have gotten horrible reviews on this website where she advertised her dogwalking service.

She may have missed some deadlines for her grad school-related test applications. Damn.

Although all those were made lighter by the fact that she heard from Mom that tomorrow was the day to go out and collect food, water, and hunt animals to be made cured meats. She could go out again. She was not sure about hunting animals though.

Her mind was wandering off to the snow-covered world out there when she heard some commotion; sounds from the main hall. She tried to focus on listening, and she was almost sure she knew what sounds those were: Wailing, sobbing, shouting.

Something had gone wrong. She grew uneasy, and stood up. The heartwrenching sounds became louder as if there were more people were wailing.

Something had gone terribly wrong.

She had just started walking to go out of the library, when Tristan came at the entrance.

He looked pale, sweat drenched his forehead, and a mix of anger and defeat ravaged his eyes.

"Tristan? Wh-what is wrong?"

She stepped closer in small, unsure steps, to Tristan.

As she got to be about half an armlength from him, she could see it. Dark red spatters on Tristan's face. Her gut feeling said that it was not some sort of paint.

"Tristan?"

Tristan shivered like he was cold. He struggled to catch his breath, and he whispered,"They died, Alanna. I failed to save them."

"Tristan? Who-who died?"

Tristan shivered, his blue eyes lost its captivating gleam, and he bowed his head when he answered,"My soldiers and I were helping these villagers, Alathyrians, to escape their village and come here to the dragons' lair. Some of them are family members of people who are here now ..." Tristan breathed faster. "We have planned everything, we moved in the dark of the night, in all quietness. But today we were ambushed by the giant crows who brought with them Thyrra's forces."

Alanna's hair stood on its end.

"We fought so hard. It was a bloodbath, a chaos. In the end, out of a hundred villagers, we only managed to bring back here thirty." Tristan's breath became slower, and he continued,"They chased us, and it was the enchanted forest that made them go round and round and lost their way. We got back here to Knyra and the dragons' lair."

Alanna stood stiff as her brain processed what Tristan had just told her.

"My people-they are dead, Alanna. I fail again and again. Is it crazy, Alanna? To want to save them? Bring them here? But instead I bring them to their demise."

Alanna shook her head. "No-Tristan, listen. You are ... a king. You do what you think is best for your people. To try to save them from the perils of Thyrra's reign of terror."

"She has been capturing men young and old and forcing them work in hard labor camps to build warships for her forces. The women and children have to work to collect whatever food could be found in the cold lakes and forests for her and her forces. She is evil and my people are the victims everyday, Alanna."

"And she is my aunt, a twin of my-my birth mother, Tristan. I don't know if my life twists could get even more strange, more tragic ..." Alanna whispered with a sense of disbelief.

"She has nothing to do with you, Alanna."

After that, Tristan fell silent. His broken heart was displayed in his eyes, and the sorrow that ate him from inside was in his trembling lips.

Alanna was not sure how, or why, but she found herself stepping closer to Tristan, and Tristan stayed still. She went ahead, tiptoed because he was so tall, and circled he arms around his shoulder. She hugged him, closed her eyes, and fought not to cry.

Tristan was surprised by her hug, he stood for a moment before his arms finally moving up and hugging her back, resting his head on her shoulder.

"It is a scary world out there, Alanna," he bowed his head and whispered directly to her ear.

Alanna nodded, her tears—no matter how hard she had been trying to hold them—rolled down her cheek.

Tristant tightened his embrace and whispered one more time,"I am glad you are here. You remind me of what's possible, a sane, peaceful life, with books and woodcarving ... a life that I thought I have left behind, but you remind me that that life is never truly gone."

Alanna lifted up her head and let Tristan wipe her tears.

"You will go home, Alanna, you will. I do not know how, but I promise you I will help you. You will go home to your dogs, to your-your beastie besties, to your grad school dream."

Alanna let go of her hug, and nodded. "Thank you, Tristan. I hope—I hope all will be better here. You are a good king. You are the true king of Alathyr, without your throne now, you are still a king in the heart of your people, and the dragons. I-I ..." Anthor has prophesied about you and me, Alanna could not say it out loud though.

Tristan still looked gloomy, and took a deep breath. "Stay here if you want. I have so much to deal with now."

Alanna nodded, wiping the last drops of tears from her eyes.

Tristan stepped back without taking his gaze off her. His lips moved like he was trying to say something, but nothing came out. Then he turned around and left the library.

Alanna felt it. A knot in her stomach, like someone punched her. It came down to her in a form of cold sweats and thumping heart. A bad premonition.

This is the beginning of more sorrow and nightmare. That was all she could her herself saying, and her tears fell again, much more than just now.

Lady Eilin's words replayed in her mind in a more ominous vibe."Anthor told me his prophecy. The king, Alanna ... the king's fate. His majesty's rise or fall. It will depend on you."

Chapter 12

He had worked since he was a teenager in the service of the royal family. His father was a member of the previous king's council of advisors. He had been allowed to sit in their meetings since he was 18, as an observer. He had spent all his waking hours learning various knowledge branches: astronomy, mathematics, astrology, diplomacy, battle strategies ... all. He had given his life to the service of Alahyrians' kings. He did not have wife or children. They would just be distractions, that was what he firmly believed in. His life was for Alathyr. Only Alathyr.

He, Carrus Akoras. He was the one, as a young advisor, who had pushed for the late queen, the mother of King Tristan, to request baby Alanna to be removed, to be whisked away-far away. The late queen, almost losing her mind in grief after the death of her husband, did precisely that. House of Evara was shocked to realize their daughter's secret scandal was known by the queen, and pushed their daughter to throw away her baby whom they believed in all their heart and mind to be bad luck, a curse of Pan, their beloved god and divine master.

He did it all. He had to protect the kings' family, his obligation was to the goodness of Alathyr. A baby, born on a winter night, out of a proper grace by Pan, could not be good news to this land.

Now that wretched baby was back as a young woman who seemed to have won the heart of his master, King Tristan. That could not be.

"I will make sure King Tristan is safe. This land is so dark now. I have to do something to destroy that wretched girl!" Carrus grabbed his dagger and stabbed it to the wood table in front of him, the only furniture he had in his tiny cubicle a few doors down from the king's library. The table cracked by the force of his stab. His eyes were red from anger, and his forehead was wet from his sweat. A shadow crept within his heart, and owns it more and more.

The night had grown late when Alanna finally went back to her parents Garlan and Hanna. The main hall was still alive with crying families and some wounded villagers and soldiers were tended there too. Mom was busy helping the wounded, and she did not see Dad anywhere.

She decided to help Mom and Lady Eilin who was busy preparing medicinal herbs to help with the wounds.

Her heart sank everytime she heard loud wailing of families when their loved ones lost their fight against the wound and passed away.

Lady Eilin patted her shoulder, and nodded her encouragement at her. "You do not have to stay in this hall, Alanna," she whispered.

Alanna thought for a bit, she saw Mom busy with calming a crying child who had bandaged of her arm, and Tristan was holding an old man who cried like a baby. He had lost too many family members tonight.

But before Alanna could say anything, from the corner of her eyes she saw a woman shouting and charging at her. She turned to see her, and the woman, a middle-aged burly woman, arrived at her spot, slapped her, and grabbed her shoulders.

"Go away you monster! You are the bad luck! Bad omen! Evil! You cause the death of my son tonight!" she screamed and cried at the same time. Her strong hands threw Alanna on the ground and started choking her.

Alanna tried to scream but she could not breathe. Her legs and arms flailed wildly, she managed to grab the shoulders of the woman who was choking her and tried to pry her away from her.

Then she saw Lady Eilin jumped behind the woman and grabbed her. The dragon healer yelled and threw the woman to the side. Anger burned in her eyes. "Don't you dare touching my daughter or calling her bad omen anymore! Nothing that is happening now in Alathyr is her fault! Nothing! Don't you dare!" she screamed on top of her lungs. For a someone whose health was weakened, she showed much strength. Her breath was fast, her eyes burned with anger, her fists clenched like she was ready to fight. She would take no bullshit about her daughter.

"She is my beloved daughter. I have given my life, my dream, my love ... all ... for the dragons, for Alathyr," Lady Eilin fell to her knees and spoke with tears on her cheek. "All I ask is to be with my daughter, please let her stay here in peace. Please. All of you. As a mother, I beg you."

The sight of Lady Eilin kneeled in front of hundreds of eyes in the cavernous hall, begging the people to let her stay in peace here touched Alanna to the core of her heart. She brought herself up to a sitting position and struggled to breathe normally. Suddenly loud roar of the dragons filled the hall. The floor shook. The dragons and their healer had telepathy link, they had felt Lady Eilin's sadness and anger and were affected too.

Alanna crawled and hugged Lady Eilin. Her tears fell and Mom rushed to be with them too. My two moms, she repeated to herself. Maybe it was never about choosing which life she wanted, which Mom she'd rather be with. It was never about having to choose. It was about having them both in her life; two women, strong in their own ways, who loved her. What else could she do besides being brave too?

She saw Tristan in the far side of the hall, stared straight at her. She nodded at Tristan to tell him she was alright.

She felt something else though. From the corner of her eyes, she felt someone was stabbing her with such hatred, cold, look. She turned her head slowly, and she saw Carrus standing with glaring eyes right at her.

Lady Eilin held her tight for some time after the raging woman was pulled away by some soldiers and the situation had calmed down. She cried in soft heave, and Alanna hugged her back. Mom and Dad sat around her in silence. It was obvious that Mom was trying to give Lady Eilin the time and space to be with her. Though deep worry creases appeared in her adoptive parents' forehead, they kept quiet and it was only their deep gaze at her that showed her how much they cared and worried and sad about what had just happened.

"I will be okay, dear mothers and dad," she let out a loud sigh and tried to smile. It pained her to see so much worry on those people she cared so much about.

Lady Eilin let go of her embrace, Mom and Dad nodded in unison. They all looked at her and Alanna nodded. "I am fine, now all of you. Please. Go rest. I demand you all to go rest." She was trying to break the heaviness with a light joke, but the three did not seem to get it. They thought she was serious and they looked at one another. "We are going to sleep. Don't worry. Are you coming too?" Mom asked.

Alanna was not sure she wanted to go to bed now. Her heartbeat still raced way too fast to be able to sleep. "In a bit," she smiled. Lady Eilin smiled finally and patted her shoulder. "I will be off then, would you come see me and the dragons in the morning?"

Alanna nodded. Lady Eilin bid her goodnight and went away to check some of the people she had treated for wounds. Mom and Dad hugged Alanna one more time and they too left.

Alanna just sat there in the middle of the cavernous main hall. The wounded had been treated and they were resting on makeshift cots and blankets, their family stayed close to them.

She did not see Tristan anymore that night. After all the tragedies that had happened tonight, he must have been busy trying to contain the damages.

When she went back to her cubicle, her parents had fallen asleep. She laid awake the whole night. She could not sleep. Not with so many strange things that had happened to her.

Chapter 13

Alanna went to visit the dragons and Lady Eilin early in the day, the moment she heard some movements and some gentle roar downstairs, she was on her way.

She spent a bit of time with Lady Eilin; being brave enough to pet the dragons was her accomplishment that morning. Rannathor was the one that she patted, the other three (or the boys as Lady Eilin referred to them) were unsure. They stood farther away, tilted their head, and just stared in a slightly concerned, slightly amused at their precious little sister Rannathor being patted.

Rannathor was enjoying the interaction with Alanna; she purred and shoved her massive head to be patted by Alanna, and Alanna touched her head. The scales felt rough on her hand, but the girl dragon's eyelashes that grazed her hand felt soft, like dog fur soft. Her big eyes opened and closed a few times along with purring sound that got louder, and Alanna could not help but chuckle. "You remind me of Chester," she whispered to herself. Rannathor's eyes widened like she was wondering who Chester was, and the girl dragon nodded her head gently. For the first time, Alanna felt comfortable down here with the dragons, especially with Rannathor next to her.

After that, she went upstairs and Lady Eilin followed along. The morning had crept up and the main hall was buzzing with activities. And that was when she heard the news: The plan for some representatives of the families to go out and find food and water was cancelled in the light of what had happened last night. Only soldiers and some men who would go out and tried to find as much food as they could and brought them all back.

It was the last straw for her. She had been looking forward to look at blue sky again, and yes, even the snow and cold air. She shook her head. "I want to go out!" she cried. "Please let me come with you guys! Come now!" she begged to a group of soldiers who were ready to go. She was going hysterical, she knew it.

The soldiers looked at one another. "We cannot bring you, Miss. It has to be with the king's permission ."

Alanna sighed, her mind went calmer now and she understood the soldier's position. She really did not want to be any trouble. "I understand, sir. I am sorry I was rather hysterical. I didn't mean—"

"Surely His Majesty will not have a problem with one more person joining? She will not be any trouble. I guarantee," Alanna did not finish her sentence, turned, and saw Lady Eilin smiling at the soldier.

"I do not know, my lady. I-I do not want to get in trouble."

Lady Eilin nodded her understanding then she winked at Alanna before rushing to farther corner of the hall and found the king there, well, cornered the king was more like it.

Alanna held her breath and somehow she wished her birth mother would not do it—went and talk to the king about her wish. She watched Lady Eilin speak to the king, and Tristan said something back, and the dragon healer started animatedly talking back. The king seemed to think for a moment before he finally nodded.

That was it.

That was how she ended up in the group that went out from the dragons' lair. Groups of men with carts filled with empty barrels to be filled with water and other equipments to collect food.

Tristan made her promise that she would always stay close to him. Groups of soldiers went first and secure the forest areas where they would go. This time they would go to the forest around a lake, a few kilometers down south from Knyra and the enchanted forest that was protected by the dragons' magic and telepathy.

"I am sorry. I don't mean to be any problem," she quietly whispered when they were outside already. She had taken a few minutes just admiring the frozen waterfall Knyra, while Tristan coordinated tasks with his men.

"Your mother, Lady Eilin, is not the easiest to say no to, no matter that I am the king," he whispered back. "Now please, stay close to me. If you get hurt, I think the dragon healer herself will tear me apart limb by limb."

Alanna wanted to smile, but Tristan looked serious. Their eyes locked for a bit, and finally she could see a faint smile on his lips.

She listened to her order. She stayed close to Tristan, collected some tree barks as instructed by Tristan—he showed her specific trees that had these barks, the specific look of the barks that would be useful for them, and how to carefully cut them. These barks could be made to be healthy soups and medicines.

The soldiers were in groups that spread out and did some hunting and managed to kill some deer and caught some fish in the cold water.

She finished her bark collecting duty after three big bags of barks were collected and Tristan said that would be enough. She was careful to always watch where Tristan was. She tried her best not to be in the way, but to be outside was just so relaxing, so refreshing.

She ran around, extending her arms like she was an airplane, enjoying cold wind on her face, she did not care so much that the sun hid behind the clouds. Being outside was enough of a treat for her. Winter's cold did not bother her at all. Lady Eilin had let her borrow her thick jackets, a wool beanie-like hat, and thick snow shoes.

Now she was just busy making her snowman. It was easy enough with so much snow around.

"What is that?" Tristan suddenly came kneeling next to her.

Alanna looked up, smiled, and realized the small snowy plain was quiet. All the soldiers and other people from the catacombs were still spread out doing their duties.

"Snowman! Come now. You have never played with the snow like this?"

Tristan watched her snowman in all seriousness. The round big snow ball for the body, the smaller snow ball for the head, and now she was working on the two protruding round legs. "No," he answered.

"Here, you can put the eyes," she shoved two black round-ish gravels she found by digging in the snow to Tristan.

"These are gravels."

"No. They are eyes. For the snowman."

Tristan watched the gravels, then he carefully set the two gravels on the snowman's head.

"Like that?" he asked, and the seriousness in his voice made Alanna laugh. Being outside did help much with her mood, her heart felt lightened though all that had happened to her still lurking at the back of her mind like a monster that was ready to strike back anytime there was a chance.

"Perfect!" she laughed, put her right thumb and index finger together to form an OK sign though Tristan did not get what it meant.

Tristan became quiet, his expression turned pensive, and his captivating eyes looked so blue now in contrast to the snow around them. "Your laughter-it is beautiful," Tristan spoke and startled Alanna.

Alanna was speechless at first to the compliment before she took a deep breath, something from her memory of the past came resurfacing again, the leftover of a laughter disappeared from her face. "There was a man who also said that my laughter was beautiful. His name was ... Jake. He made me believe I was pretty, I was not a boring nerd who buried my nose in books and dogwalking." Alanna distanced herself from the snowman and sat on the snow. I hate you so much, Jake!

Tristan looked confused at first, then he sat next to her.

"I gave my heart to him, and he betrayed it. He said my laughter was beautiful, quite a few times he said that. But he betrayed me anyway," Alanna continued as-a-matter-of-factly, her right hand was scooping some snow, made a little ball of it, and threw it to the snowman. Over and over again.

"What made you think I am like that man?"

"I just don't believe in compliment by a man anymore."

"I am sorry."

"For what?"

"For complimenting you."

Alanna did not know what she had to say. Honestly she loved the compliment, but she also did not believe it. She was just confused. "You must have broken a lot girls' heart," Alanna was not sure why she said that; she guessed that deep within her she was holding up a hope now that Tristan was not Jake, Alathyr's version.

Tristan stared at her with confused gaze. "Why did you say that?"

"You are a king, not bad looking. A great archer."

"I have never-never broken any girl's heart if you must know. I am too busy with my duties, and books. And wood carving." He sighed and continued half whispering,"I do take offense that you think I am like that-that Jake."

Tiny snowflakes floated around them.

"It is snowing. We have to go back soon."

Alanna nodded. "Tristan, I do not mean to compare you to Jake. I am just not over his betrayal I guess. I pretend I was done with it in front of my parents, but—"

Those blue eyes widened, and Tristan took a deep breath and looked up to the falling snowflaked before opening his mouth to say something again, "Betrayal is not something you can get over quickly. I understand that."

Snowflakes fell harder and they could hear their groups coming closer. It was time to go back underground. She stood up, wiped some snow from her face, and Tristan stood next to her.

Alanna started walking when she felt her hand was grasped by Tristan. She stopped, and turned around. Tristan grabbed her hand gently and pulled her closer.

"I have this gut feeling, really strong one, that my life will someday depend on you, Alanna. I do not know how or when or why it will be that way. But in any case, just so you know, if that happens, I believe in you. I believe my life is safe in your hands."

Anthor's prophecy. Alanna was going to shout it out loud, but she could not.

"I do not want you to get hurt, Tristan. I want you safe," she shivered. That was all she wanted to say to Tristan, her whole feeling, her whole being, her whole heart. From the depth of her heart, she wanted him safe, unhurt. He was definitely not Jake. Not even in the slightest. Her heart had decided that.

Tristan pulled her closer, and she knew it was maybe the most incomprehensible deed she did today, but she caressed Tristan's jaws, tiptoed to make up for her shorter stature, and hesitated. It was Tristan's eyes, trained on her—gentle and inviting—that convinced her that it was alright, like he knew what she wanted to do, and he gave her permission by staying still.

She closed her eyes, brought her face closer to Tristan, and pressed her lips on his.

Tristan's lips was cold, but it warmed up soon enough as he answered her kiss with deeper, hungrier kisses hot enough to melt her in his arms. His arms tightened around her back and waist, he pulled her even closer, so close she could feel her breasts pressed against his solid chest. She could hear his heartbeats, faint and busy as her hands moved to caress his broad shoulder, and made a trip down to his back and that was enough to make him groan.

As snowflakes kept faling around them, their world turned warmer, entangled within each other's embrace. It was an unseen force that pulled them in, ravaged them with flames of honest desires and wishes of the heart; to be one, to be together.

Chapter 14

They pulled apart from each other when the noises of the group coming to their direction was becoming louder. Then Tristan was busy making sure all was ready to go, and they moved fast.

The rest of the trip back home was surreal at best. Alanna could feel her whole body warm despite the snowfall, and she dared not looking at Tristan. She had just kissed the king of Alathyr. And that felt good. Really good. Should she tell Lady Eilin? Mom and Dad?

Wait. Is Tristan a boyfriend to her now? The way they kissed just now are definitely not friendly peck on the cheek. So what exactly are we now? You didn't think of that before you kissed him now, did you, stupid Alanna? Those questions sent her almost into panic, her eyes found Tristan but he was ahead and busy talking to that advisor of him, Carrus. She tried to breathe, to calm down. It's getting complicated, she told herself. The fact was this, and she was sure of it: She did like Tristan. A lot. Otherwise she would not have kissed him. And she was certain by now that Tristan reciprocated her feeling. That was good. Good, if they lived in her universe across the Pan's door, a universe where they could fall in love and do stuff like couples do without worrying about the dragons, her bad luck status, that sinister advisor of him, Carrus, and yes, the fact that he was a king with all the obligations and entitlements that followed such a majestic position.

Alanna bit her lips. She did not want Tristan to get hurt because of her.

The groups traveled with their carts, and each men in the groups carried a large basket like a backpack on their back.

They had to walk closely when they entered the enchanted forest area, and Tristan showed them the way. Alanna made sure she followed, and she knew Tristan followed her every move to make sure everyone got to the Knyra, and into the dragons' lair again.

The night had fallen when all carts and the groups had gone inside the underground settlement.

It was just Tristan and her outside of the gate. They stood admiring Knyra, the frozen waterfall that now gleamed in moonlight.

"Alanna, tonight is full moon. Have you seen a winter full moon from the peak of that small hill behind the enchanted forest?" Tristan smiled under the moonlight.

"I don't think it's safe now, isn't it? To be out there at night by ourselves?" her heart beat fast.

"I have done it a few times, to have a quiet time for myself. I know a quick route," Tristan whispered. "From here, we go on the edge of the forest, from there we cut through the eastern part of the forest, then the hill was there."

Alanna bit her lips, thought for a bit. Tristan did not take his eyes off her, and he looked so handsome under the moonlight.

"If you do not wish to go, it is alright, too—"

"I want to go. It sounds beautiful. Winter, hill, and full moon."

Tristan nodded, extended his hand to her. "Come!"

Alanna took Tristan's hand, and they started walking on the edge of the enchanted forest across from Knyra.

They kept walking until they got quite far away from Knyra. The thick snow did not hinder them, tonight was special for them because it felt like a date night. A night when they realized their feeling toward each other was not going to waste. They started running in choppy steps because the thick snow made running almost impossible, and when Alanna fell down, her face got into the snow, and Tristan pulled her. They sat up on snow, under the moonlight, laughing in hushed voice. Tristan pulled her closer and started kissing her again.

Alanna forgot all about the complicated situation that could arise if she got into a relationship with Tristan. She just wanted to be with him tonight. That was all. She could deal with the world later.

They embraced each other, and when they let go, they kept their forehead touching, and Tristan whispered to her,"There is something I want you to have ..." he then took out a wood bracelet that he had always worn.

"This," he whispered as he slid the bracelet to Alanna's right wrist.

"You made this?" Alanna admired the smoothness of the bracelet. The wood was dark brown-black, and it looked sturdy.

"My first ever carving. I learned how to carve, and this was the first work I completed. I was just fifteen at that time. Have always worn it till now."

Alanna caressed the bracelet. "It's so beautiful. Simple, strong, beautiful bracelet."

"Simple. Strong. A circle like bracelet—it means eternity in Alathyrian's culture."

Alanna gazed to the blue eyes a few inches from her. "Thank you. I won't take it off."

Tristan kissed her one more time, and grabbed her hand. "Let us move again!"

Alanna smiled. Then she felt it. Like a punch in her stomach. Something heavy and sad that came bulldozing at her. Fast and unpreventable. The two of them had been happy the past few hours. And too much happiness was not good because sadness would sure come right after.

Anthor's prophecy. She wanted to stop and tell Tristan about it, but she saw how happy he was, and she could not bring herself to do it.

Maybe tonight they would stay happy. No sadness. Nothing. Maybe it was just her and her anxiety and her trauma after all the strange things that had happened to her these days.

Maybe she was silly to even decide this early, but she was certain of it: She had fallen in love with Tristan.

She hoped they would be alright. Alright, and happy, and together.

They kept walking and at some point Tristan took her into the enchanted forest, and he knew the way in there.

They were there for a bit, chatted in hushed voice, then they got out of the enchanted forest, and sure enough, there was a small hill close by. The massive winter moon looked like it was perched on top of the hill.

Beautiful and cold.

Carrus knew he was good at something, other than all the academics stuff, all the stuff he needed to give advice and lend wisdoms to the king: He was good, very good, at throwing his tiny dagger and killing a rabbit point blank. That was his hobby since he was a child; practicing his dagger throwing to the point of perfection, a sort of obsession for him, a channel for his violent bursts of rage that had haunted him since the day of his boyhood when his father regularly hit him till he was unconscious. He was raging at his father, but he dared not even looking at his eyes, red like a drunk monster. He took it out on dagger throwing, and he imagined it was his father's face that he threw the dagger at. He grew so good that he never missed any target.

He would not miss tonight too.

He had been following his master, the King, and that wretched girl for some time now. He was careful, very careful but he was very much helped by the fact that King Tristan was not careful. The two lovebirds only cared about each other, they never looked back, to him who was following them in gentle steps and watchful eyes, especially when they went into the enchanted forest.

He would kill that bad luck woman. The only way to save the king from its dark grasp, and Alathyr from more bad luck. He had prepared it all: A dagger, tiny, painted exactly like the dagger used by Erebus' forces so they would be blamed for this. He already knew where he would sneak into hiding when his deed was done, he had changed his regular clothes and cape to the ones coloured all white to camouflage himself better in the snowy region. He had paid a handsome amount of money to some of his most loyal followers to lie when asked where he was tonight. He was with them, always. He had this planned out. The king asking Alanna to go to the hill provided him with a way to carry out his plan. His majesty becomes stupid and careless because of love, he told himself.

Carrus nodded, his eyes shone in brutal rage.

They were out of the enchanted forest already, and he followed from behind some old trees.

They stopped to admire the moon from where they stood, close to the base of the small hill. That was his chance to throw his dagger right at the head of that bad woman.

He took out his dagger and was ready to throw it so as to not miss a chance because the two lovebirds would walk again soon.

But his dagger suddenly fell from his hand like someone had pried open his grasp on it, and his whole body grew weak, so weak that he fell on his knees and he could see the king and Alanna walked away further. His vocal chord was also not working—quiet, limp, and voiceless.

He went into panic because breathing became much harder for him like someone was choking him with invisible hands.

He knew someone stood behind him. Very close he could hear the breathing and he could smell faint flower fragrance—a mix of lily and jasmine.

He could not stand up, his legs turned jelly-like, so he turned his head, and his eyes widened in shock upon seeing who it was that stood behind him, incapacitated him, and choked him through invisible hands.

"You ... why? How—" he heaved, struggled for air to breathe.

"Stay away from them. They are mine." A gentle, lilting voice. Melodic. Deadly.

Carrrus shook his head in fear and struggled even harder to breathe. Severe pain was etched in deep contorted grimace of his face, and that was not for long. He let out a hoarse yelp, like a mouse getting crushed by a much larger predator, and a crack was heard.

The crack was followed by Carrus' body fell and slumped on the snowy ground, his neck twisted in an awkward angle, his eyes opened wide in terror, and fresh red blood streamed out of his nose and mouth. Death had welcomed him in an eerie silence.

Chapter 15

Alanna gazed at the silverish moon with darker spots dotted its massive surface with awe. The moon looked like it was perched by some divine hands on the top of the hill.

"It is beautiful—" she whispered to herself.

Tristan stood half an arm-length from her and did not say anything. He was just staring at the moon too.

When Alanna glanced at him, she realized how mournful he looked.

"What is it, Tristan? You look sad."

"I am happy tonight, Alanna. And I am sad because I feel that this happiness will end. This happiness with you will not last."

Alanna understood that completely. It was like this whole world they were in and their situation were not the kind that would allow long lasting happiness. It could not be. Lasting happiness and evil that lurked in every corner—those did not add up. One had to give way to another.

"Let's-let's just go back, Tristan. I have seen the moon from here. We do not need to go up the hill."

Tristan's hand found hers and grasped it tight. He agreed.

But it was when Alanna tried to turn around and walk away that she realized she could not move her body. Her body began to feel like a lump of jelly. No strength whatsoever. She fell on the ground and her tears flowed like streams of river from her eyes.

"Alanna? What happen?" Trustan kneeled next to her and grabbed her shoulder, but she could not open her mouth to talk. Her mind went blank. She saw Tristan's expression changed from calm to surprised to horror when he threw his gaze behind her.

"There are—there are creatures coming, moving fast. Alanna, come, we have to go!" Tristan tried to carry her, but it was then that a strong, cold wind blew and he was thrown at least twenty meters farther from her.

Alanna wanted to scream but she could not. Her vocal chord, her whole body, all was weakened to the point that she could not will herself to do anything.

Then Alanna smelled it. The smell of flowers, flowers that reminded her of Lady Eilin, a mix of lily and jasmine. The smell got more intense, and now she felt like someone stood behind her. But she could not turn around and see because she just slumped on the snow without any strength to get up.

She saw dark shadows moving fast, closing in on Tristan who had stood up again.

It is not fair. It is not fair. Tristan and I were happy just now. I know it's going to end, but so fast? It's not fair! Her body shook with silent cry and heavy tears that fell.

The dark shadows took shape, materialized to be four creatures—creatures from the pit of hell would be the best way to describe them because they were definitely not human beings. They were snake-faced human-bodied monsters. Erebus' monsters. They were slender and tall, at least 2 meters in height, and they wore black armors with sharp teeth of steel protruding from the surface. A gold ring circled their snake head. Each bore a weapon; a long sword with a glistening tip.

The four hissed and surrounded Tristan, and he was ready with his sword that always hung in its scabbard on his belt.

Alanna wished she could just die at that moment so she did not have to witness whatever it was those beasts were planning to do with Tristan. It could not be benevolent deed anyway.

But she was still breathing, albeit heavy and her throat and nose were choked by tears. Her body slumped and she struggled to even move her toes. Snowflakes drifted around her. Whoever stood behind her let out a high-pitched yell and the four beasts started attacking Tristan.

And she watched it as Tristan fought the four beasts.

He was a skilful swordsman too in addition to be a superb archer.

But the four beasts were also good at swords, and they moved quickly, like shadow that flew around Tristan, materialized, attacked, and moved again. They were an efficient war machine if such a term should exist; brutal, fast, and skilled.

Alanna felt fingers, cold and frozen, touching her temple. Then she saw black powder being poured at her, it fell from her forehead, to her nose, and mouth. She struggled to stay away from it but she could not move. She inhaled the black powder, and the first thing she notice was that it smelled like a mixture of ashes, blood, and steel. The powder was coarse enough to grate the inside of her nose. She grabbed a handful of snow to help withstand the discomfort.

The moment the powder entered her body, she could feel changes in her.

Her vision began to blur, the world seemed to slow down and grew quiet in her head.

Her mind turned empty, blank, as if a new page had been turned and she had to refill it again. Through blurry eyes, she saw a battle between a man and four beasts, she convinced herself that she knew the name of that man. That man was important to her, that man-but what is his name?

There was a name, and it had just dissipated like grains of sand that escaped from the gaps between her fingers.

Her mind became so dull she forgot what the name of the man was—the man who were fighting the four beasts and now clearly was losing the battle.

Her tears kept falling, however. Tears was the last one to go, that much she knew.

And as her vision turned from blurry to dark, the last thing she saw was this: The man, the one who was fighting the beasts, the one whom she could not remember anymore who and what his name was, he lost his sword, and he fell on his knees with the four beasts closing in on him.

Her heartbreak was complete. She lost her consciousness with tears still rolling on her cheek.

Chapter 16

She woke up from what seemed like an eternity of sleep, or even worse, like she had just escaped from the grip of death. Her head was heavy like some horses had just trampled on it. The inside of her mouth was dry, and she could not swallow because of it. Her eyes hurt though she could see where she was.

She was in a room, on a large bed with four black wood pillars from which hung a white lace-embroidered net. The room had stone walls, dark grey and cold. Across the bed was a small, square oak table and on top of it was a ceramic jar and a ceramic glass, and two dirty grey armchairs on its left and right. That was it. The whole room was just so grey. From one large window covered with thin curtain to her left, she could see snow falling. She would venture to guess it was early morning from the way the light was—the grey light that may have been from the sunrise that was covered by fog and winter clouds.

As her brain sputtered to life again, she realized something that sent shiver down her spine.

She existed in this bedroom, she could touch everything, but she had no idea who she was. What is my name? How did

I get here? She wanted to scream out those questions, but to whom?

Her breathing began to go faster when panic embraced her. She had no memory whatsoever.

"Ah, you are awake," soft melodic voice startled her, and she turned to the direction of the room's massive oak door where a woman now stood. She was tall and slender, with large, honey-coloured eyes and raven black hair. Her dress was a silk long-sleeved, blood red top with tight bustier that showcased her plump cleavage and black laced long skirt. She was beautiful, her skin looked so pale it seemed like it was glowing. Her raven black hair was long reaching her waist, loose, and straight. Her whole body exuded flowery fragrance, a mix of lily and jasmine; fragrance that smelled like a contradiction to her, it was as if she had smelled the same fragrance in a calm situation in her life, and in a fearful situation. She had seen the woman's face before, she did not remember how or when, but she did meet that woman before.

"Who are you? Where is this?" she asked questions, and continued,"Who am I?"

The woman at the door smiled—a strange, awkward smile. "I will tell you all. You need to know all." Then she sauntered closer to the bed, and sat at the edge of the bed. "Are you ready to listen, sweet girl?" she asked while twirling the tip of her long black hair.

A nod from her was all that woman neeeded to start telling her more information.

"Your name is Alanna. You are my daughter, my long lost daughter. My name is Thyrra, I am the queen of this land of snow."

She gasped. "My name is Alanna," she repeated. "And I am your daughter."

Queen Thyrra nodded and patted her hands. The queen's hand was cold, so cold it sent shiver down Alanna's spine. In fact she had trembled quietly since the moment the queen stepped into this room. She did not understand why, it could also be because it was now winter as she could see snow from the window.

So her name was Alanna. She was a daughter of that woman in front of her, a woman who claimed to be a queen of this snowy land. She repeated those new facts to herself, and somehow failed to convince herself about the truth of those facts. But who else could she ask about her?

"Call me Mother, Alanna. I would love to hear it. I will tell you all about what has happened. So listen to me now," Queen Thyrra's eyes trained on her, and her heart beat so fast it seemed like it almost exploded. Something about the queen, her mother, that scared her.

Alanna froze.

"Are you scared of me, sweet girl?"

Alanna was quiet, she was not sure what the safe thing to say was. She could not stop herself from trembling.

The queen stood up and went to the wood table. She poured a brownish liquid from the ceramic jar into the ceramic glass and brought the glass to Alanna.

Alanna could smell herbs in the drink and she hesitated to take the glass from Queen Thyrra's hand.

"Drink it. It is your medicine, called ivara. It will help you calm down and listen better to me."

"I am not-not thirsty."

"Yes, you are thirsty."

Alanna shook her head, too weak for the queen to care. The queen extended her left hand, and touched Alanna's forehead. Alanna felt the coldness of that hand transferred into her skull, the coldness that dulled her thinking even further, and she lifted her hand and took the glass.

"Drink all of it," Queen Thyrra smiled though her eyes did not smile. In fact her whole face looked stiff like she was made of wax. No creases of wrinkle or blemishes of anything. Just tight and smooth and frozen. Alanna somehow knew the queen was not the same age as her, or older than a middle-aged woman. But it was like a veil covered her face, the face she saw now was just too pretty, too unblemished, too perfect.

Alanna's hand trembled so hard she could not find her lips at first. Her tears for some strange reason started flowing. But she drank the liquid, the medicine called ivara. It tasted bitter with a hint of ash at the end.

The empty glass fell from her hand to the floor and the ceramic shattered.

Her mind did calm down. It was like a blank slate that was ready to be filled. She stared at the queen, and the queen nodded her approval.

"Good girl, Alanna. Now listen. I am Queen Thyrra, your mother. Our land, Alathyr, has been in nightmare for some time now—"

Alanna sighed in her struggle to catch her breath again.

"My twin sister, Eilin, has staged a treacherous coup a few months ago, and poisoned the dragons, our treasure, with her black magic, and put them captive in a place protected by her evil sorcery. With the help of our beloved god, protector of our land, Erebus, I manage to protect the throne of Alathyr."

Eilin. Dragons. Alanna faintly remembered those, she did not know how and what the details were, but she knew she had heard about Eilin and dragons before.

"Eilin has always wanted everything I have. I had the love of your father, Bragan, and she loved him too. She killed him in a jealous rage. I am the dragon healer, the caretaker for the dragons, and she wanted them too. She is a crazy, raging evil sorceress, Alanna."

Alanna's head hurt. Something inside was fighting whatever information told to her by Queen Thyrra. Too many holes in the queen's story, she just could not pinpoint exactly what. Who am I, really? she screamed in her mind.

"This kingdom, the throne, the dragons, are all mine, Alanna. You are mine. Eilin wants to take all away from me, the way she took away Bragan, the love of my life, from me. I will kill her, Alanna. I will kill the dragons too because they have fallen too deep now in the abyss of Eilin's darkness. Lord Erebus will help me as always."

Queen Thyrra sighed and for a moment it looked like she was about to cry. "Eilin and I used to be close like twin sisters should be. We even like the same fragrance: lily and jasmine. We look the same, we smell the same. Then she took everything from me, robbing me of everything and everyone that ever mattered to me. This is my revenge, Alanna. I vow to rob her of all that ever mattered to her and I will serve my lord Erebus' wishes at the same time." Then the queen stared at Alanna again, this time she did not look like she wanted to cry. She looked plain steely, with bubbling rage that floated just below the surface of her face.

Fear crept up even more on Alanna as she sat up stiff. Her mind had been busy fighting whatever it was the queen was saying for reason she did not understand, but now it grew quieter from fear.

"Now, Alanna, a chambermaid will come and help you get dressed. You may then get acquainted with this palace. Then ... I will need your help in something." The queen examined her face with such focus that Alanna turned her head aside.

"Wh-what help?"

"Ah. Be patient. You will figure it out soon enough."

Queen Thyrra smirked, that and the secretive tone of her sentence made Alanna even more uncomfortable.

The queen caressed Alanna's cheekbone before taking her leave.

Alanna sat up on the bed, fear and confusion swirled like a tornado in her mind. Who am I, really? she asked herself again. Then her eyes saw on her right wrist: A simple wood bracelet. Dark brown-black wood bracelet. So simple it had escaped the attention of Queen Thyrra.

The bracelet was a simple, sturdy bracelet, there was nothing special on it except that it made her feel safe, that it had come from a time that even though she could not remember now, but it was a time when she was loved. That bracelet was a message of love for her, from someone, from a time that she could not find any trace of it in her mind now. Her gut feeling told her all that, and at this moment of confusion and fear, she decided to believe it.

She grasped the bracelet tight, brought it to her lips, and kissed it. Who am I? Who gave me this bracelet? Do I have someone who love me, and whom I love? Who am I?

She began to cry, and the bracelet was soon wet from her tears.

Chapter 17

The chambermaid, a burly woman of about fifty, stiff, unsmiling, and almost as cold as the queen, came to see to her needs a few moments after Queen Thyrra left the room.

She wore a large, round bun of her hair on top of her head. Her hair was grey, almost the same color as her clothes. Her arms were disproportionately thinner than what would be expected from her body size.

She did not talk much at all. She grunted and nodded at Alanna as a greeting and Alanna mindlessly nodded back. Her hands were then busy wiping tears from her cheek, she did not wish the chambermaid to see it.

"Here are some clothes for you, my lady," the chambermaid placed a stack of purple, dark colored skirts and blouses on the corner of her bed.

Alanna did not like the colors of the clothes. Too dark for her taste. But she kept quiet.

Her head still felt heavy and dull pain pounded the inside of her skull, but the chambermaid only cared about making sure she carried out her duty well, which was to get Alanna ready.

She helped Alanna coming down from the bed, then started helping her with her clothes. The clothes she wore was not new and looked much older and ragged than the ones provided by the chambermaid.

In the end, she stood with her new clothes in front of a mirror brought by the chambermaid. She insisted her wood bracelet be left alone and the chambermaid looked at it with disdain and shrugged her thick shoulder.

She wore long sleeved silk purple blouse with a purple jacket on top of it, thick black wool long skirt, and her hair was braided to the side. Those colors of blouse and skirt made her look pale. Her lips was chapped from the dry weather, and her eyes had lost its vivacious shine since—she was not sure since when. The chambermaid asked if she wanted to color her lips a bit with a mixture she brought; a red paste like stuff she put in a small wooden box. Alanna shook her head. She did not want to look pretty.

After she was done helping Alanna, the chambermaid went out and came back with a tray of food. Plain bread and some sort of warm drink. She set the tray on the table and nodded at Alanna, then she left with the ceramic jar from which Queen Thyrra poured out the ivara for her to drink earlier.

Alanna did not touch the food or the drink, partly because she was not hungry, and partly because she did not find the food or drink appetizing at all. She still wondered what it was the liquid she had drunk earlier. It made her mind weakened and she listened to the Queen's story about her without the ability to critically appraise it. Her mind just went blank.

Her headache subsided a bit, though her head was still heavy. Her clothes was not comfortable at all, and in the end she decided to pull one of the armchairs and sit by the large window which was locked, staring at the snow-covered clearing which she would guess was some sort of backyard of whatever palace she was in now. There was a high wall, about 5 meters in height, made of blackish mountain rocks and a gate made of welded metals that separated the palace ground from the forest behind it.

She sat and stared at the snowy landscape. There was not much to see. The back yard was not like a proper palace garden, curated and maintained by a team of gardeners. It was more like a haphazard evergreens bushes weighted down by snow that grew here and there. A few oak trees dotted the landscape. That was all.

Her mind was tired, and she felt numb. Every few minutes she would look down to her wrist and check the bracelet to make sure it was still there. It was, and that calmed her down.

So many questions laid dormant in her head now, she knew she had lots of them but she could not articulate them, let alone actually asking them or finding someone she could ask questions other than the queen.

She did not think the queen was her mother. That was for sure. But who was that woman to her, then? How come her face feel familiar to her but she also felt that she did not know her?

Her eyes may be playing trick on her because just now she thought she saw something moving in the snow. The snow moved. That cannot be, silly girl, she reprimanded herself.

But it moved. Something was moving toward her.

She focused on the snow and realized something was indeed running toward her.

It got closer.

It was a dog. A three-legged dog, to be exact.

It got next to Alanna's window by now and Alanna could see it: The dog had snow white fur, striking light blue eyes, and a long bushy tail. Its front right leg was missing.

The dog jumped up and stood on its hind legs, putting its only front paw on the window.

"Hey..." Alanna tapped the window, trying to see if she could open it. The window was deadbolted.

The dog was calm, and Alanna felt that the dog knew her. She tapped both of her palms on the window, the dog licked the window, and stopped, and its gaze now focused on Alanna's wood bracelet.

The wide eyed stare at her bracelet made Alanna realize: The dog might know about the bracelet.

"Hey, do you know this bracelet?" she asked to the dog. She was not even sure the dog could hear her, but it started licking the window where her wood bracelet was.

The dog kept licking the window as if it wanted to get to the bracelet, it wanted to be with it, and looking at that, Alanna was certain: The dog knew something.

"Tell me who I am—" a desperate plea to a dog, but Alanna did not care. She tapped the window gently, the dog stopped licking and now staring at her with such gentle glow in its blue eyes. It bowed its head, the looked up again at Alanna.

"I've seen you—" she whispered to the dog, and that feeling got stronger. "I am sure I have played with you. But who are you? Where did we meet?" she shook her head.

Suddenly the door's handle was turned from outside.

Alanna gasped and the dog understood, it ran away at a speed that astonished Alanna.

"What was it? A fox?" the chambermaid came into her room. No smile as usual. Just a question that sounded more like an investigation.

"A white-white fox. Indeed," Alanna answered.

The chambermaid stood still and watched her like she was trying to ascertain the truth of what she had just said about the white fox. Across from her, Alanna stood still and stared back at the burly woman with a new found sense of determination. She was not sure where it came from, but she would not be stared down by that woman.

"Do you have a problem?" Alanna cocked her chin and asked flatly.

That surprised the chambermaid. She stepped back and shook her head. "I came to bring you to Her Majesty the Queen, my lady."

Alanna sighed, she knew full well that she could not just run away. She had no idea where she was and where she should go. Her heart rattled in fear, but that burly woman in front of her pissed her off enough by now that she vowed not to show how scared she was in front of her. She nodded.

The chambermaid showed her outside her room, and she was led to corridors made of beautiful granite, with floor covered in red carpet. Paintings hung on the walls, she was not sure paintings of what because she kept her gaze straight ahead.

Guards stood at the entrance of every corridor. Black banners hung on some parts of the wall, large and ominous.

Alanna's heart sank deeper because she knew she was now taken to something, or somewhere, bad. Really, really bad.

Chapter 18

Alanna stared ahead as the queen brought her to a smaller corridor at the end of the long walkway next to the side garden of the palace. She did not even look around anymore as she walked. She just stared ahead, trying to psych herself to be braver, stronger.

She kept walking and her brain was not processing anything, it could not. Her mouth was dry, and she knew the night had fallen outside. The small corridor was dim, only lit by some torches on the left and right.

At the end of the corridor was a door, painted black and made of sturdy, rough wood.

"Come. I need your help in something important," the queen who had been walking two steps ahead of her now turned around and smiled at her. The smile sent shiver down her spine though. It was more like a grin, a smirk, like the queen had hidden a bad thing, thought she was smart about it, and tried to hide it with a smile.

Queen Thyrra took a key out from her skirt pocket, and opened the door.

Alanna's knees shook so hard she almost fell down.

"Come," the queen nodded at her.

Alanna breathed fast and stood still.

"Alanna, I say come."

Alanna took a couple deep breaths and followed the queen into a small corridor behind the door. She did think in a flash of thought of trying to run away, but that thought died down right away along with the fact that her knees were too shaky to even walk solid steps, let alone running away.

The corridor was dim, with only a couple torches light the way. It was much colder in here than outside the black door and the smell of moss and dust invaded the nose. Alanna began to cough when the smell became so intense it made it hard for her to breathe. This corridor had not been opened much at all so it seemed to her.

Their walk ended at the top of a winding stone stairway.

The queen stopped, turned at her, and smirked. "It is dark down there. Be careful with your steps."

Alanna did not respond. She is not my mother, she screamed within her mind. There was no way this scary woman was her mother. No way. She did not want it to be that way.

Who am I? that question pounded her again as she made her way down the winding stairway, the wall around her only had just enough space for her to half-extend her arms left and right.

Why do I feel like I do not even belong here? In this palace? In this whole snow-covered place?

The stairs kept winding, and Alanna did not even count anymore how many winding of the stairs that she passed by before they got to the bottom of the stairway. She tried to focus on her steps, making sure she did not tumble down as the queen walked a few steps in front of her. Her mind was empty, she began to think of something-something simple, like her meeting with the three-legged white dog earlier. But even that was difficult for her.

The smell of damp rocks and moss became much stronger, and there was another door right in front of them. Another oak door painted in black with two torches on the wall to its left and right.

There were two guards posted there.

Alanna let out a shriek.

The guards were not human.

They were snake-faced human-bodied monsters, slender and tall, at least 2 meters in height, and they wore black armors with sharp teeth of steel protruding from the surface. A gold ring circled their snake head. They stood stiff with their unsheathed sword crossed each other, forming an X on the door.

"They-they—"

"My beloved guards. Loyal. Quiet. Deadly."

"They are not human."

"Of course not."

The queen nodded at the guards and the two nodded back, taking away their swords from the door.

Queen Thyrra took Alanna's hand, grabbed it, and made her walk the last few steps to the door. Alanna dared not looking at the two beasts guarding the door.

"What is behind that door?" Alanna shivered as she asked the question."Your task."

"Wh-what task? Queen Thyrra—"

"Call me Mother. That is an order."

Alanna stayed quiet. She could not mutter that word. Mother. Not to the woman in front of her; wax-like beauty with no warmth whatsoever. That was not an image she had in mind of a Mother. Whoever she was, whoever her mother was, the woman in front of her was not her mother. She was certain of that.

"You will call me Mother, Alanna. I will wait. It will happen. Now, come."

Alanna did not speak again and she kept her eyes to the door. Though she could still smell the body odour of the two guards; they reeked of decayed flesh—like some dead animals that had been left out in the open air on a warm summer day and their body was infested with maggots. Her stomach churned. Is that how monsters smell like? Disgusting creature. She swallowed her saliva, trying not to vomit.

The queen took a key and opened the black door.

She stepped in, and Alanna too.

The room behind the door was a half-circle room, with rough rock made up the walls and round-ish ceiling. A dungeon of some sort.

There was one giant torch placed on some sort of a rock platform. The flame from the torch shone to give dim light to the room which was not that big.

Two tree logs were placed in the middle of the room. The tree logs went from the floor of the room to the ceiling.

The logs were where a man was tied up, one arm chained to each log.

He was shirtless, and his dark wavy hair covered his face. It was obvious he had been tortured, scars of lashing were seen on his chest and stomach. Dark red and purplish lines, silent witness to the lashing that he had endured.

Alanna froze, it was like a massive wave of memory about to break through the wall in her mind, the one that prevented her from remembering who she was, or what she was before she got stuck with Queen Thyrra.

"He—he is..."

"His name is Tristan. A commander of evil Eilin's soldiers. He is an assassin who has killed so many of my people. A bloodthirsty demon. My guards had managed to capture him and since then he was chained here."

Alanna repeated the name in the silence of her mind. Tristan. Do I know him?

The man called Tristan slowly looked up and his expression changed upon seeing Alanna.

"Tristan! Ah. You are awake. You have shown commendable strength in withstanding the lashing from my guards. Now here, let me introduce to you—" Queen Thyrra walked closer to Tristan, grabbing Alanna's hand.

"My daughter. My sweet daughter, Alanna."

From the closer distance, Alanna could see him better. Dark blue eyes that now focused on her with a mixture of shock and confusion. Rugged, stubby moustache and beard forming shadows around his chin and jaws. A black tattoo that looked like a long, sharp claw ran from his left temple to his left jaw.

"Alanna..." he whispered. There was dried blood on the corner of his lips.

"Listen, Tristan. I want you to tell me how to get to Eilin and the dragons. You have the map of the enchanted forest in your mind. Draw me the map. You have refused to do so despite lashings so now my daughter will ... motivate you to do as I wish."

Tristan shook his head. "How dare you, Thyrra! Evil witch!" he shouted and started thrashing about to try to let himself go from the chain. "Don't you dare hurting Alanna!"

Alanna was confused. Why did Tristan, the assassin, the bloodthirsty demon care about her safety?

"You do not have to pretend to care about Alanna's safety. You had almost killed her in the past, remember? I want the map. I want to kill Eilin and the dragons that have turned to be evil like her! I have to do it for the safety of all in Alathyr!" Thyrra spoke slowly, carefully, making sure her words were heard properly by Alanna.

"Liar!" Tristan thundered.

Alanna's head hurt so much it felt like it was going to explode.

"Alanna is my daughter. How could I lie to her?"

"Alanna is not your daughter! She is Eilin's!"

"You have been so blinded by Eilin's sorcery, demonic Tristan. Alanna is mine. The daughter of Bragan is mine. My one and only love, my dear Bragan."

"Alanna! You are in danger!" Tristan trained his eyes on Alanna, shouted at her.

But Alanna could not think about what she needed to do. Being next to the queen had always made her so dull. She just stood, and tears began to crowd her eyes.

"Alanna, ask Tristan to tell the map to go to his group. The rebel. I will come every hour and bring your ivara drink, your medicine for your health. If you refuse to drink your medicine, Tristan will be lashed. The drink will help you listen to me better. Be a good daughter to me."

Tristan shook his head in fury.

"I will give you time till sunrise, Alanna. Make him talk. If he still refuses, I will make him watch as you drink the whole jar of ivara, let your soul be mine as my daughter forever, then your hands will execute Tristan, and I will attack the whole region of the forest with Erebus' forces. I will not care anymore that there will be Alathyrian civilians on the way there. I will burn them all. It is an important sacrifice for the good of this kingdom."

With the ominous threat, the queen left Alanna in the room with Tristan.

"Alanna, please remember who you are," Tristan spoke with heavy breath as he withstood his own pain. "You are Alanna, the daughter of Eilin, our dragon healer."

Alanna stood still. Her mind sputtered to life a bit now that the queen had left the room. "What are you talking about? Are you going to hurt me?" she trembled and took a couple steps back.

Tristan's expression turned gentler. "Hurt you? How could I?" he lifted his head more, grimaced in pain, stared straight at Alanna as fresh blood flowed from the corner of his lips, and he spoke half-whispering, "Alanna, I am Tristan—" he grimaced again, "And I love you."

Chapter 19

Alanna stood in silence and let Tristan's words sink into her consciousness.

I love you. Even in her current state of mind where everything blurred and she could not remember anything, she knew what that sentence meant. Instinctively she glanced at her bracelet, a bracelet her gut feeling had always insisted to her that it was given to her by someone who loved her.

It did not make sense. How could it be? If Tristan loved me, how could he be chained there? But isn't he an assassin?

"I made that bracelet, and I gave it to you just shortly before Queen Thyrra and her Erebus' forces attacked us."

Alanna kept staring at the bracelet, trying to calm herself down. Her body shook gently when she ended up breaking down and crying.

"Alanna, please-please listen to me."

"I do not know anymore. Who am I? Who are you? Are you a killer? A bloodthirsty assassin? Why do I have to listen to you?" she looked up and stared at Tristan through her tear-stained eyes.

"That bracelet, look at the inside part. There is a tiny crack, it looks like a tree branch with three twigs grow out of it. I made a mistake when I was carving it and it showed there."

Alanna stood still.

"Alanna, please. We have a big problem. Thyrra will come every hour to make you drink ivara. The more you drink this poison, the more you will listen only to Thyrra and the less chance you will have of ever remembering again everything about who you truly are." Tristan groaned in pain after he finished his sentence.

Alanna shut her eyes tight, and opened it again, took her bracelet close to her eyes, and examined the inside part.

There was indeed a tiny crack. It did look like a tree branch with three twigs grow out of it.

"Thyrra said you almost killed me..."

"Thyrra is evil. She is the twin sister of your real mother, Lady Eilin, the dragon healer. She has lied to you!" the chain crinkled as Tristan seemed to try to free himself from his shackles.

Twin. Alanna shut her eyes tight. It made sense. She had always felt like she had seen Thyrra's face, she knew it even in her state now. A feeling, a familiar premonition, a nonverbal cue that told her: She had seen that face though she could not tell when and where.

Tristan groaned again and his breath got heavier. Alanna walked closer to him and stood an armlength from him. She felt a sense of calmness of safety from him, those she did not get from the queen.

"If you don't tell me the map to go to your group, I will end up drinking all the ivara and forget all about you. I will be the one executing you," she stated all the facts she could remember.

"I cannot tell where the dragons and Lady Eilin are hiding, Alanna. I cannot do that."

Alanna shook her head. "I do not want to be the daughter of Thyrra, to serve her, Tristan. I do not want to kill you."

"Do not drink the ivara, Alanna."

"They will lash you if I do not drink it."

"It is my duty to endure it, Alanna."

"No. No. That cannot be. Tristan, that cannot be."

"We do not have much choice. Our only hope right now is that if help would come soon enough."

"Isn't there any other way? For me to drink ivara, but still not completely forgetting who I am?"

Tristan sighed, grimaced to withstand the pain, and gazed at her. He gasped an answer, "I-I do not-not know, Alanna."

A tug in her heart, a tint of warmth, a tinge of gentleness that had begun to engulf her when she looked at Tristan made her believe even more: Tristan was the one to be trusted.

She stepped closer, and carefully touched Tristan's face. Gently she lifted his chin, and Tristan's blue eyes welcomed her with all the pain that he had to endure.

"You said you love me—"

Tristan nodded. "The night Queen Thyrra and the beasts came to attack us, we were together. We kissed with all the passion in our heart. I have never kissed a girl before. You are my first, and my only, Alanna."

"We have-have something together-something beautiful, something happy, haven't we?" she asked while her trembling index finger caressed Tristan's lips, wiping the blood from the corner of it.

Tristan let out a heaving sound, and nodded.

"I do not remember all that has happened when Thyrra and her beasts came to attack us. But I remember this feeling. Warmth. Gentleness. You." Alanna caressed Tristan's cheek and her tears rolled down her cheek in glistening balls of water.

"Do not drink the ivara, Alanna. Please. Let me take the lashing."

"Do one thing for me, Tristan."

"What is it?"

"Everytime after I drink ivara, tell me a story about us. Whatever little things you know about me, tell me. Kiss me. Remind me of you, of myself, of us. Will you do that?"

"Alanna, no—"

"Tristan, do you trust me?"

Tristan heaved and his body swayed. "I do, Alanna. I do."

"Tristan, listen. I will take one sip of ivara everytime the queen comes in here. It will spare you of the lashing—"

"Alanna, no."

"I can handle this. I can. And I hope help would come soon before you die through my hands and I become the servant of Thyrra."

Tristan looked at her, and Alanna realized more and more how much those eyes, that gaze was familiar to her. I know you, she repeated that with full conviction.

"I believe that you are not an assassin. You are not a bloodthirsty monster. I do not remember what you are. What are you...?" Alanna shook her head. She could not remember what Tristan was. What was his duty? His position? His role?

"That will come to you. It is not important now what I am."

"Trust in me, Tristan."

"I do, Alanna. I trust you with my life."

"Will you do as I said?"

Tristan looked at her unblinked for a moment and answered, "I will."

They stared at each other and realized they had nobody else they could rely on at that time. They only had each other.

The time was up.

One hour.

The door was opened from outside and Queen Thyrra came inside with a jar of brownish liquid and a small ceramic cup. One of the Erebus' warriors came with a whip on its grasp.

The queen stood in the middle of the room, her chin cocked up, and her right hand held the cup into which she had poured some ivara.

Alanna shook her head, indicating she had failed to make Tristan talk.

"My Lord Erebus' warrior has even brought a special whip for him, the one with steel on the tip so he could feel it better. So, would it be lashing for him? Or drink for you?" the queen lifted the cup. The Erebus' warrior whipped his lash on the floor, making such noise that rattled Alanna enough that her knees trembled. She could see tiny steel thorns on the tip of the lash.

"I will drink."

The queen smirked and handed her the cup.

Alanna did not look back to Tristan, she just took the cup and drank the ivara liquid in one gulp. The liquid went down her throat, warm and bitter with a hint of ash-like substance within it. She wanted to vomit it out, but she swallowed it back. She could not risk Tristan getting lashed by such a brutal whip.

The queen snickered and nodded. "Very good, my daughter Alanna!" with that she turned around and left with a warning, "I will be back in one hour."

Alanna stood still after the queen and the Erebus' warrior left. Her mind started to be blank again, all that she had just done with Tristan before the queen came into the dungeon began to fade away.

"Alanna! Please come closer. I have things to tell you. About your real mother, Lady Eilin, about the dragons, about us ..."

Alanna shook her head hard, trying to gather some concentration. She willed herself to walk closer to Tristan.

"Alanna, listen-please listen to me. Let-let's start with my name again. I am Tristan ..." then Tristan began to tell her: About Pan's door, her life in the other universe, her dreams of going to grad school in psychology ...

"Psychology? Grad school?" she felt like there was an open box suddenly handed to her, a box of nice surprises and she got to open it. The box was named Dreams. Her heart tingled because somehow, in her subconscious mind, those words were once her familiar words.

"Yes, Alanna. You explained to me what those meant. I still find it difficult to wrap my mind around those terms, but it's your dreams. I am happy for you."

Her head hurt, like something from her subconscious mind was trying to push through an unseen barrier and be remembered again .

"Tell me more ... Tristan ..."

Tristan grimaced in pain, and told her about Lady Eilin, her real mother. The dragons: Anthor, Drathor, Selivor, and Rannathor. Each with their antics and endearing characteristics.

"Rannathor," she repeated, for some reason she found that was the most interesting to her.

"Yes. The girl dragon. She has a special soft spot in her dragon heart for you, Alanna. Rannathor."

Some frozen ice thawed in her head. Tristan looked at her, and those blue eyes captivated her, and she knew it was not the first time she was captivated by those eyes.

Tristan. She remembered him. Yes. "You kissed me before. We kissed," she nodded and walked closer to Tristan.

Tristan looked up sheepishly and nodded. Then he tilted his head like he just remembered something, then he said,"And Filip, my dog, how he loves you too!"

"Filip?"

"Yes. He only has three legs. An old dog, white fur, blue eyes."

And it dawned upon her. "I saw your dog. He came to me. Filip came to see me."

Tristan's eyes shone. "He will definitely lead Eilin to us. Besides me, if anyone could find the hiding place, the dragons' lair, it is Filip. Not from an enchanted map in his mind like what I have in my mind, but from tracking the dragons' scents with his nose. He is a good friend of the dragons, the dragons allow him to track them. I have never let him tried it before, finding the way back to the lair, but Filip can. I believe in him."

"How-how far is the enchanted forest, the dragons' lair, from here?"

"A day walking. The enchanted forest regions are right outside the villages that form the outer boundary of the palace grounds."

Alanna walked closer to Tristan,"We will be fine, Tristan. Just a few more cups of ivara, and Eilin would come. Wouldn't she?"

"She is your mother, Alanna. She gave birth to you. I have never seen a mother who is not fierce and courageous when it comes to her child's safety." Tristan paused, and continued,"Listen, let me take one lash or two. It—"

"No."

"You are stubborn. Do you know the risk you are taking, drinking ivara every hour?"

"Do you know what those steel thorns do to your skin?"

"Yes. I will heal from those wounds—"

"Or dead. I can handle Thyrra's poison. Just-just keep reminding me of all that is good in my life, Tristan."

The chained king sighed and was left speechless.

Queen Thyrra came as promised, hour after hour. Alanna took the drink and staggered to Tristan after the queen left.

Tristan would tell her all, again and again. After a few cups, Alanna was weaker and in a last ditch effort to keep remembering, she started embracing Tristan. Tristan would whisper his love to her, and she would whisper it back because that was what she truly felt, and she would not ever want to forget that. That real emotion, real warmth did wonders in helping her keep her own identity, her memory.

Chapter 20

The night crept with excruciating slowness, and Thyrra came every hour with her jar of ivara poison.

Alanna drank every cup, though after some cups, she grew weaker and it became more and more difficult for her to keep any information that Tristan gave her. Tristan would have to repeat things over and over, and Alanna would kneel on the cold hard floor, crying, holding her head, trying to remember.

While the queen's dark mind grew more and more impatient. Finally Thyrra came with just the last few drops of the poison in the cup, two Erebus' warriors stood behind her. She walked to Alanna, whom by now had grown weaker that she could not stand up to walk properly.

Tristan watched her with deep sorrow, and Alanna knew the queen walk behind her, and she looked straight at Tristan and mouthed,"Trust me."

"This is the last few drops of ivara. Tristan, your choice. Do you want to tell me the map to the dragons and to Eilin? Or do you let Alanna drink the last drops of the ivara?"

Tristan stared straight at Alanna, the battle that raged in his heart and mind was displayed on his expression, and

Alanna kept mouthing, "Trust me" to him without the queen noticing.

"I-I will not draw the map."

"Ah, Tristan. Your message is clear but your voice is trembling. What kind of a beast are you? Letting the love of your life take all the poison? Alanna will forget you. Her hands will kill you. Do you know that?"

Tristan heaved in pain and agony, but he remained silent though rage flamed in his eyes when he looked at Thyrra.

"Fine. Alanna, take your last sip."

The queen now walked and stood in front of Alanna, handing her the cup with ivara.

Alanna glanced at Tristan who had grown weaker too. I hope I am doing the right thing. I hope I can remember you, and all that you have told me when I take that last sip. Tristan, I love you. She said it all in her mind.

She took the cup from Thyrra, glanced at Tristan one more time and saw that he shook his head at her. She closed her eyes, she wanted to cry, but she knew that was of no use. Please Alanna, you have to remember all that Tristan has told you, she begged to herself.

This is it, she sighed. She drank the whole cup empty.

Thyrra cackled, her unblemished face looked taut like it was going to tear apart. Her smile turned uglier and uglier.

Alanna slowly stood up and faced the queen.

"Alanna, how do you feel?" Thyrra ran her fingers—with long, pointy, painted black nails—along Alanna's jawbone.

Alanna did not answer though her knees trembled.

The deafening silence filled the dungeon.

Thyrra walked around Alanna, and when she was back in front of Alanna again, she stared deep into her eyes.

Alanna let out a groan, her knees stopped shaking, and she stared straight back at Thyrra.

"Mother."

Just one word came out from her mouth, more like a whisper, but Tristan heard it and he cried out. "Alanna! No! No!"

Thyrra roared in happiness, her arms outstretched and pulled Alanna into her embrace. "You are mine! Mine! You will stand next to me in the battle with Eilin. Eilin will see that I have taken away the only important person in her life. I win! She took my dragons and my Bragan, I take her daughter!"

Tristan thrashed about trying to free himself from the chains, and he howled Alanna's name over and over again.

Thyrra let go of her hug and Alanna stood more solid now.

"Guards! Bring Tristan to the courtyard of the palace. Alanna will execute him!" Thyrra cackled, and continued,"Then we will attack the whole region of the enchanted forest. We cut all the trees! Kill all the villagers there! They are victims of Tristan's refusal to share the map with me! The map was the benevolent way, but Tristan chose the bloody way. So tonight-tonight you all can feast on fresh blood and meat!"

Erebus' warrios let a loud roar that shook the whole dungeon.

Tristan did not protest anymore. He grew quiet, and his eyes widened, trained on Alanna. His sorrow was displayed there. His soul was crushed and broken when he saw Alanna in Thyrra's embrace and his body went limp from his heartbreak.

The two Erebus' warriors unlocked Tristan's chains from the tree logs. Then they chained Tristan's hands together.

Alanna stood still next to Thyrra, it was impossible to tell what went on in her mind at that moment.

I have been hearing voices. Murmurs again. At first I thought it was a hallucination. But the more ivara I drank, the more obvious the murmur. I am sorry Tristan, I am sorry I did not tell you because I really did not think it was anything important. They were just murmurs, it could be the effect of ivara on me. I was so drugged by ivara that I could not think properly anymore.

But those murmurs have turned to words, and it was too late to tell you because I had just drunk the last sip of ivara and Thyrra was with me.

Words, Tristan.

It said:"Alanna. Alanna. Listen. This is Rannathor."

The girl dragon, the one who has been so sweet to me.

"Alanna, stay strong. Remember us. We are coming."

Tristan, they are coming. I called out Mother to Thyrra to buy us some time. Thyrra would have had you lashed till death right there in the dungeon if she did not get anything she wanted: the map or myself as her daughter.

Tristan, my real mother, Lady Eilin the dragon healer, and the dragons. They are on their way. I hope they will be here on time.

Alanna kept the whole discourse in her mind as she walked a step behind Thyrra as they went out of the dungeon, with Trustan followed behind her, two Erebus' warriors walked to his left and right side. One of the beasts held the end of the chain that locked Tristan's wrists.

She stared straight ahead, the best way to keep her pretense that she had lost all her memory and she had accepted Thyrra as her mother.

It pained her to see how broken Tristan was, but she knew she could not look at him for a long time or her pretense would be discovered by Thyrra.

They walked now outdoor, snow all over the scenery though it was not snowing anymore. They walked on a long walkway with arches made of mozaics of stone, and they passed some soldiers which all bowed their head in obvious fear to the queen and the beasts of Erebus.

Alanna's heart beat loud enough for it to form an echo in her ears. She was scared. *Am I hallucinating? But it was Rannathor that spoke to me—wasn't it?*

Her head was heavy, and she turned around, her eyes locked with Tristan. The brokenness in those ocean blue eyes sent her breathless with sadness. She could not cry otherwise her pretense would be blown and they would all be dead. Thyrra was too happy to care. There was a spring in her steps, and Alanna would like to keep it that way. Happiness ensured the monstrous queen kept her guard down and that was what she needed: An evil queen that was engulfed in happiness, too happy to pay attention.

Alanna ... we are coming.

She had to stop herself from looking up the sky. Her eyes darted to the sky in discreet move, looking up in a quick glance. Nothing.

They arrived at the courtyard—a round space surrounded by rock pillars and evergreens that grew haphazardly on the snowy ground. One thing that she noticed as they walked here now was this: How quiet this palace was. No maid was seen, no palace staff of any kind, and the human soldiers were posted on the palace grounds, while the Erebus' warriors were guarding the inside of the palace. The palace looked dilapidated and damp with smells that invaded her nose, smells of the Erebus' warriors. The whole place reeked of death and decay.

Her eyes caught something moving among the rock pillars.

A three-legged white dog ran out from the shadow the pillars. The warriors of Erebus who were guarding Tristan was taken aback at how fast the dog was charging at them.

"Catch it!" Thyrra shouted. "It is Filip, Tristan's dog! That wretched dog! Catch it and kill! How come is it here?" Thyrra started shouting again while the two guards ran around trying to catch Filip.

Filip was fast and nimble, it ran around and did some tricks that caught the two snake-faced beasts off guard. It ran fast with three legs and that was enough to give Alanna a sliver of courage. She shot a glance at Tristan, and Tristan caught her eyes. She winked, and Tristan understood.

Thyrra shouted in anger, and called for more guards. More snake-faced foul smelling beasts came running from different posts in the palace area.

"Eilin is coming! The dragons are coming! I can feel it! Be ready!" Thyrra ran around and looked up to the sky.

But Filip managed to create distraction with its speed and tricks.

Alanna, we are here!

Along with the voice that seemed to come from within her head, Alanna heard a loud thundering sound from above. The sound was like a hurricane that was passing through, ravaging all in its path.

Alanna looked up and she saw four majestic dragons flying fast from four directions, homing in on them. The loud hurricane-like sound was the sound of their massive wings flapping. Each flap brought gusts of wind on the ground.

"Arrows! Shoot them all!" Thyrra bellowed.

The snake-faced beasts hissed and took out their bow and arrows.

The dragons sped up, diving in from above to them.

Tha largest dragon, Anthor, arrived first, and stabbed its claws into the chest the guards next to Tristan, destroying their body on the spot. He then scooped up Tristan, and brought him flying.

Alanna ducked down and saw the other three dragons attacking the snake-faced beasts. Mercilessly the dragons grabbed them with their sharp claws and hurled them to the stone pillars. The evil guards stood no chance at surviving such powerful hurling—their body pretty much destroyed on impact with the hard pillars.

Alanna crawled on the ground among the commotion and grabbed a dagger that fell from one of the dead Erebus' warriors.

"Come, come my daughter!" Thyrra grabbed her hand while her eyes were busy watching the dragons.

Alanna never hurt anyone before in her life, but now, now she had to do it. She knew it. She took her dagger and stabbed the hand of Thyrra."I am not your daughter!" she screamed.

Thyrra turned to her with rage that sent tremble down Alanna's spine. She stood up and backed away with the raging queen chasing her.

"I will kill you all!" Thyrra shouted.

Alanna's back hit the rock pillar. Her mind went so fast, struggling to figure out what to do to escape with so little time; Thyrra began to charge at her like a wounded lioness.

Alanna, duck!

Rannathor spoke to her, and she looked up. The girl dragon dived to her from behind and Alanna knew what to do. She ducked and Rannathor swooped in from behind, directly to Thyrra. Her claws pounced Thyrra, but it did not kill the queen because the queen managed to jump away. Thyrra fell on her face and Rannathor turned around and landed in front of Alanna.

"Thanks, Rannathor!" Alanna shouted and Rannathor's eyes winked a few times.

The beasts started shooting their arrows and Thyrra chanted a spell that brought in the giant crows to the courtyard.

Come. We fly!

Alanna stared at Rannathor, was not sure what to do. "I don't even know how to ride a horse, let alone a dragon," she muttered to Rannathor.

Come! Or you will be dead at the hands of Thyrra! Rannathor insisted.

Let's fly!

Chapter 21

Thyrra staggered to stand up and began to get ready to charge again at Alanna's direction. That convinced Alanna to jump onto Rannathor's scaly back and hang on to dear life as the dragon took off.

"This is crazy! Rannathor! Are you sure?" she was not sure why she asked that but as the wind blew on her face and her feet lost touch with the ground, no seatbelt, no airbag, nothing, she freaked out. She flew on the back of a dragon for goodness sake!

I have never flown with a human on my back. I will try my best! Hold on tight!

"That's very calming. Thanks, Rannathor!"

Rannathor swooped down and Alanna screamed, the girl dragon was avoiding some red arrows that began to be shot from Erebus' beasts on the ground.

I may not be as big and tall as my brothers, but I always win when we play flying games! My smaller body helps in maneuvering on the sky!

"Great, Rannathor! We need all the flying skill you have!" Alanna was clutching Rannathor's horns so tight while her legs clutched both sides of Rannathor's belly. She opened her eyes and she saw mess. Down there, she saw another woman, a woman who led some human soldiers in fighting the Erebus' warriors. The woman looked just like Thyrra, and she was fighting Thyrra.

Your mother, Alanna. Our Lady Eilin, our dragon healer. Filip showed us the way and she has led us here in silence, getting all human soldiers who have served Thyrra out of fear to be on our side again. She comes for you. Being a mother means being a warrior too!

Alanna's mind became clearer, and she nodded, patted Rannathor gently. Arrows kept coming and Rannathor proved her maneuver skills. Alanna screamed till her throat hurt but that did not bother the girl dragon. She kept watching as Eilin and Thyrra fought down there and showing such masterful swordplay.

A loud thunderous roar came from the northerly direction and Alanna saw Anthor with Tristan on its back.

Tristan had his bow and arrows and started shooting the beasts on the ground with his arrows. Alanna knew of course that Tristan was a master archer, and he did shoot so many of the beasts on the ground.

Suddenly Thyrra chanted a spell so loud Alanna could hear it though she did not know what it meant.

Eilin was thrown on the ground when she tried to grab Thyrra. She stood up, and Thyrra kicked her one more time.

The spell brought change to the Erebus' warriors. Their eyes glowed red and their bow and arrows also glowed red. They moved faster and their arrows seemed to be alive, finding their targets with almost as if they had a mind of their own.

Alanna watched with horror the tide that had turned on the ground. Anthor with Tristan on its back, Selivor and Drathor started having difficulty in maneuvering against the arrows.

Rannathor was busy too, but the girl was good, really good at flying—her thinner, more slender body helped in the maneuvers. Alanna began to get used to flying on a dragon, she needed to try to follow the direction of Rannathor's move, while holding on tight to the horns and clutching her legs on Rannathor's stomach.

Alanna could see Eilin fight Thyrra again but she fell down a few more times. It was more than obvious that she had been wounded by Thyrra. She kept mouthing No when she saw her mother, Eilin, having a hard time defending herself down there against her twin. She shook her head when Eilin fell again and Thyrra charged at her in ruthless move.

Then when Selivor got stabbed on its left wing by an arrow, Drathor lost its focus and also got shot by an arrow on its tail. The twin dragons roared in pain and crashed on the ground and Erebus' warriors began to swarm around them.

My brothers! Rannathor screamed in Alanna's mind.

Alanna watched when Anthor also got shot and fell on the ground with Tristan quickly jumped down from its back before it hit the ground and now he was fighting the beasts with his sword.

The three wounded dragons must now defend themselves against the swarm of Erebus' warriors. They swished their tails left and right, and used their arms to start plucking the beasts and threw them away. That strategy worked only so far. The three grew weaker and the swarm of the evil got closer and closer to their body.

The human soldiers were also busy fending off the attack from the giant crows. The blackness of their feathers filled the sky and their squawking was deafening and arrows were shot by the soldiers to bring them down.

Alanna! Lady Eilin is injured now. You are our healer! The cry of Rannathor echoed in her mind. Rannathor with her exceptional maneuvering ability was safe so far and busy plucking beasts from the ground and slung them far away.

"It's just us two girls now, Rannathor. Be strong," she whispered to Rannathor.

The three dragons on the ground roared and looked up to the sky, to Alanna. Then they bowed at her.

And Alanna heard it, the voices of all the dragons spoke in unison in her mind.

Lady Alanna, we trust you with our lives. You are our healer. Please heal us. We trust you.

Heal us.

Lady Eilin is too wounded to heal us now.

You are the dragon healer.

Alanna shook. "Rannathor? Do you hear that?"

Yes, Alanna. You are my friend, and my brothers and I have decided you are our healer. Please heal us, my brothers especially. Our king is in trouble.

Alanna saw Tristan still fighting hard against the beasts. But he wobbled from an injury on his leg, and Alanna remembered Anthor's prophecy. She understood it now: The rise and fall of King Tristan will depend on her.

"How to heal your brothers down there, Rannathor?" she shivered.

I do not know, Lady Alanna. It will come from within you.

Alanna grabbed Rannathor's horns tighter, and she could feel panic engulf her.

Those dragons on the ground, fighting for their lives against the swarm of such monsters. If they got destroyed, Tristan died, Eilin died, and Thyrra would take over this whole land. Who could guarantee that Thyrra would not become strong enough to someday pass through Pan's door along with her terrible foul-smelling soldiers, the warriors of Erebus' the demon god of darkness itself?

Mom and Dad, her adoptive parents, they would not survive Erebus' warriors. Her friends. Her dogs.

Alanna screamed on top of her lungs, and she felt defeated. She did not know how to help the dragons.

Be our friend, Alanna. That is what we need right now. A true friend in our darkest hour. Stay with us and help us heal.

Rannathor's words in her mind brought her back. Friends. She wanted what was best for the dragons, and that was all they wanted.

A friend in their darkest hour.

Selivor's painful roar made her realize what she needed to do. A true friend would not let the dragons be in pain. She took a deep breath, and started thinking of all the possible friendship stuff she coud do with the dragons.

I can see what you were thinking, Alanna. I love it. We could go flying together! We are friends.

Alanna nodded. "Friends, Rannathor. I hope my thought get to your brothers too. It reminds them of what will happen in the future! Their wounded heart and body will survive this war!"

Alanna thought of all the beautiful things in her own universe too, her dreams, her dog friends, her plans ...

What could be. Beyond today. Beyond this war with Thyrra and her evil soldiers.

These got to the dragons. The flow of hopeful thoughts helped them, perked them up and they began to heal.

Alanna kept sending the dragons all her hope, her messages of encouragement, and realized one thing: The dragons had the strength and ability to heal, all they needed was someone to remind them of it, to trust them, to be their friend, to stay with them.

"I believe you all four of you, dear friends. We are in this together!" Alanna whispered.

The three dragons thrashed about and they grew stronger. Anthor became strong enough for Tristan to ride on its back again, and it changed the tide of the war on the ground again.

The battle between Tristan's human forces and Thyrra and Erebus' forces was waged in all ferocity on the whole palace ground. Alathyrians, men and women, who had been living in fear under Thyrra's monstrous rule came in droves and started helping by throwing rocks, shooting arrows at the Erebus' warriors. They would gather on the outskirt of battleground and drag any weaker Erebus soldier down and began asssaulting it with all they had. Like that, on and on, and that helped.

Selivor and Drathor got better and started their attacks as well.

Alanna saw her mother, Lady Eilin, still fought her twin. She went down with Rannathor, and jumped off the dragon's back. Thyrra did not realize it and was still choking Eilin on the ground.

Alanna ran and jumped on Thyrra, raining her with punches.

Thyrra shrieked and turned to her, letting Eilin go.

"I will kill you!" she shouted, her rage made her wax-like perfect face turn red, and she charged at Alanna. She grabbed Alanna's shoulder and threw her on the ground, and Alanna scurried away with whatever bravery she had left. Thyrra got to her quickly enough, choked her, and dragged her up from her sitting position.

"Stop, Thyrra! It is between us! Leave my daughter alone!" Eilin rammed forward, took her dagger, and stabbed Thyrra on the back.

Thyrra who was going to kill Alanna roar in pain, turned to look at Eilin, and she shook.

"You-you..." she tried to grab Eilin's face but she fell on her knees before reaching her sister's face.

"Thyrra ..." Eilin started sobbing and she kneeled in front of Thyrra.

"We were born as sisters, we were good friends, Eilin. Until you took everything away from me. My dragons, my love Bragan. Everything."

Eilin did not cry anymore. She just kneeled and stared straight at her twin. Her tears streamed down her cheek.

Thyrra trembled. "I will never forgive you, Eilin—"

Eilin took a deep breath,"I do not need your forgiveness, Thyrra. You have destroyed so many lives because of your mad revenge. I will go on living my life, maybe I will think of you and our better days."

Thyrra was going to say something else, but only gurgling sound escaped from her mouth. Then she fell on her face on the snowy ground, and her body turned to foul-smelling dust that was absorbed by the ground and disappeared.

Eilin froze for a moment before finally breaking down in sobs.

Alanna let Eilin cry then she lowered herself, and hugged Eilin. There was no need for words, though she could not find any appropriate word to say in that moment even if she had tried to look for it.

Chapter 22

The battle with Thyrra and Erebus' warriors was done, and Alathyr was on its way of healing and rebuilding what was destroyed.

The people who had lived in the dragons' lair came back to their home, trying to put together their families, and mourning their dead because there was no family that had not experienced any loss.

Lady Eilin was wounded and had to rest to heal. The duties as a dragon healer were now passed on to Alanna, though Alanna was not officially a dragon healer yet, there was a special ceremony for that and could be done only when the previous healer had passed away.

The dragons were back in their place in the palace ground; a dome-like rock structure with round windows behind the main palace. Alanna spent more time with the dragons, and Anthor, Selivor, and Drathor had warmed up to her more. Filip survived the battle too, and the old but valiant dog spent a lot of time with the dragons, just chilling around them. Rannathor was her friend from the get go. She would come and lay next to Alanna, and through her telepathy, she would tell Alanna tidbits of information about her brothers. The girl dragon was gentle and warm, and quite chatty; something that Alanna truly appreciated. It was not exactly the same with Rannathor, but it was close enough to the girl-bestfriends vibe, something she used to experience when she got together with her bestfriends in her own universe; talking about celebrities, classes, gossips, food, vacation plans, complaints, dates, or just nothing at all. She had always been the most bookish among all her bestfriends, she always felt at home in the library, but she did love it when she spent time with them.

She was a dragon healer, at least till her mom Eilin got better. Then she did now know what would happen. Could she go back? How she wished to still do her stuff there in her own universe.

Lady Eilin did not push her to accept her right away as her mother, and that helped tremendously in cultivating trust, plus she was the one who led an army to rescue Alanna from Thyrra's grasp. Alanna appreciated the time, the slowness, the gentle approach that Eilin took with her.

Mom and Dad were supportive, they did say they would follow her whatever her decision, to stay here or to go back to her other universe."We are home here in Alathyr, but we have also built a home for us in Oakridge, Alanna," that was what they said. Tristan had helped them find a place for them to stay in the palace ground—a small cottage-like house at the corner of the side garden of the palace, a home that was occupied by the gardener before the gardener and his family moved away to a bigger house. Alanna loved the cottage, and she decided to stay with Mom and Dad. It was better that way—there were too many changes in her life now, and she loved the feeling of something constant when she was with them. She would spend her mornings with Lady Eilin at her home in House of Evara mansion, afternoons she would drop by to visit the dragons, and evenings she spent with Mom and Dad. A good arrangement for her for now at least.

Tristan was back on the throne, and her relationship with Tristan was something that had been in Alanna's mind a lot.

Where would their relationship go from here? They did have something together, and it was not just her imagining it. Their kiss happened, their time in the dungeon happened.

A relationship, something more than just friends, the whole thing seemed impossible at first but it did seem like they were in it now, she also could not just turn around and pretend it was not there.

Tristan had grown busier now that he took control of the throne again, that was why they had not gotten a chance to really sit and talk about them. In a way, she was fine with it because she was not ready to talk about it. What do I want? I really don't know! was what went through her mind over and over again.

She was torn. A part of her wanted to return to her own universe, continuing on her trajectory in chasing her dreams: She wanted to keep up with the deadlines for grad school applications, she wanted to offer a huge apology to all her clients and hope that she could continue with her dogwalking business, she wanted to be in her own place again. Another part of her wanted to stay here, with the dragons to which she had developed stronger bonds, with Eilin, whom she wanted to get to know more. Lady Eilin had not mentioned about Thyrra at all these days, and Alanna could not even begin to fathom the hurricane of emotions that must be swirling inside Lady Eilin now—

"Alanna?" Lady Eilin's voice startled Alanna who had been just sitting by the window of Eilin's room that morning, watching the snow fall again and letting her mind wander here and there. Eilin sat up on her bed, she did look much better and stronger that morning. Some color had returned to her face, though a thick cloud of sorrow still lingered in her eyes.

"Hmm?" Alanna turned around, she was sure she had a blank look on her face.

Eilin tilted her head. "What are you thinking about?"

"Well-nothing, nothing much—"

"Really?"

"Well-I don't know where to even start explaining to you."

Eilin nodded, straightened up her back on the pillow behind her, "Try me."

"Eilin, I-I am not sure what to do now, you know." Alanna took a deep breath, put together some sentences in her head again, walked to Eilin, and sat by her side on the bed. "I kind of want to go back to my universe, to chase my dreams, to do all those stuff I have always wanted to do, to do my thing—"

Eilin smiled. "Then what's stopping you?"

Alanna bit her lips, not sure she had heard that right. "I am a dragon healer, right? I kind of have to, you know, be here?"

"I am still the dragon healer, my dear daughter. The dragons have chosen you because I was wounded in battle, and you are to be the next healer indeed, but I bet you they will not mind if it is still me who is doing this duty and you go do your-your thing in the other universe."

"But what would happen if I am in the middle of the most fun phase of my life and-and..."

"And I am dead and you have to come back here?"

"Well, yeah—"

Eilin sighed, looked up to the ceiling, her brows furrowed as she thought of something, then looked at Alanna again. "How about this, Alanna. I will guide the dragons now, and I will try to talk to them, to let them have some understanding of what you want. Then when I am dead, you can still stay at your universe, do your thing, you just have to visit them. Would that work?"

Alanna wanted to hug her birth mother, hesitated a bit, then she went ahead and hugged the current dragon healer, a hug that was reciprocated with a tight embrace from Eilin. "Thanks, Eilin. Thanks so much."

"The dragons, especially Rannathor, adore you Alanna. They do. Rannathor has been doing the telepathy with you even before you are chosen by all of them to be their healer. That never happened before, you know?" Eilin's smile got wider, and she added,"Dragons may look scary with their horns and scales and wings and all. People are scared of them, but I can tell you this: They are deep down the kindest, gentlest creature I have ever met. Their long life means they have seen so much, and what they have seen, they have experienced, have turned them kinder, wiser. They understand you more than you could ever imagine."

Alanna nodded, she did not doubt what Eilin had said. The dragons, they loved her, she could feel it in every fiber of her being. Kind, old, ancient beings they were indeed.

"If I may take a guess, there is a bigger issue that holds you back here," Eilin patted Alanna's cheek gently.

"What is it then?" Alanna was curious.

"Tristan." A knowing smile, a gentle wink of her eyes, Eilin was successful in turning Alanna's face bright red.

Eilin nodded. "Tristan is a good man, and I can see how much you mean for him, his heart is yours, though you do realize he is a king—"

"What does that have to do with-with … I am not even sure what to call what I have with Tristan."

"He is the king of Alathyr, the dragon rider, the chief of the Royal House of Pryssus, the guardian of the dragons. Those titles come attached with their own risks if you do decide to go on with- well, let's call it relationship. Sounds about right?"

"What risks?"

"Danger to his life, pressure from his job titles, and the intrigues from around the throne. If you love him, those will not be a problem for you to deal with."

"I-I don't know, Eilin. I think I do like him a lot. In fact I think I do love him, that is such a big word it scares me to use it."

Eilin took a deep breath. "That's all you need to know, Alanna. You love him. I love Bragan, your father, and I knew all the risks. I took the risks, and it ended up in tragedy. But I never regret it. I am glad I have loved even though only for a short time."

Alanna could feel a certain warmth in her heart.

"Love will make you brave, Alanna. It will."

"I-I just don't know how it's going to be if I decide to go back to my own universe. How would our relationship work if we are so far apart?"

"Have a good talk with him. I cannot answer that, my dear."

Alanna thought for a bit, nodded, hugged Lady Eilin one more time, and took her leave with Lady Eilin smiled her encouragement to her.

Alanna stood in her little bedroom in the cottage. She was just looking at the window, to the snow that had stopped falling, leaving whiteness that covered the entire ground.

Mom was sewing something in the front room and Dad had not yet returned from his palace duties.

Dad had volunteered to help out in the rebuilding of the palace after the short but decisive battle with Thyrra's forces. Dad was among the workers who were fixing the walls of the palace that got damaged during the fight against Thyrra, while Mom would help out in the soldiers' kitchen, cooking and preparing food for the battalions of soldiers that had been called in to the capital to help with defending the capital and now were on their way to go back to their posts in different parts of the kingdom.

Alanna sighed, and her gaze turned to a piece of crumpled paper she had on her right hand.

She had wanted to clean up her clothes, and took the jeans she wore when she was taken to Alathyr by Mom and Dad that night. She found, stuck in the back pocket of her jeans, a graduate school brochure. She had attended a grad school fair a week before she was whisked away to Alathyr, an event where various universities came and promoted their graduate studies in various majors and specializations to undergraduate students in their third and fourth year.

The brochure was from the university that had become her favourite. Good psychology program that matched her interests, and she had met some professors there in academic conference that she attended.

Alanna nodded, she knew she had to go home, to her own universe. At least for now. She had dreams, and she could not let them go.

Epilogue

"Alanna?" followed by a knock at the open door.

Alanna turned and saw Tristan by her room door. Her heart skipped a beat when she saw him. Tall and handsome with his dark hair swept up on a bun and his blue eyes shone gently in the dim light of Alanna's room. The dark, claw-like tattoo on his face made him seem so foreign, a reminder of how different her world from his was.

"Hi-well, hello-I..." Alanna tried to act cool and that failed.

"You are nervous. Are you hiding another man here somewhere?" Tristan teased with a playful glint in his eyes. "May I come into your room? Your mother was on her way out and she was shocked to see me at the door just now but thank our god Pan she let me in anyway."

Alanna nodded, instinctively tightened her grasp of the brochure in her hand.

Tristan walked into the room with a limp because his leg was wounded in the battle. "I have been busy these days. I am sorry I—"

"Don't apologize, Tristan. You have duties to do. I very much understand that." Alanna watched Tristan's leg,"Your leg ... still hurt a lot?"

Tristan watched his leg. "No, not so much."

"Really? You grimaced with every step you took just now."

"I-I feel the pain still. A little bit."

Alanna bit her lips, debating if she should tell Tristan about her own wrist wound, then decided against it. "I hope your leg will be better soon, Tristan."

Tristan stood half an armlength from her and he nodded gently. "It will be. It is not my first battle injury, Alanna." He paused, threw his gaze to the snow outside, sighed, and continued,"I just feel it's not right ... not to have time with you."

Alanna was not sure what to say as a reply, then she decided on something. "Tristan, listen-I want to-to talk with you about something." There she said it, though words seemed to escape her thought now. She took a deep breath, turned to the window to watch the snow outside again to compose her thought again.

"Alanna? What is it?" Tristan stepped even closer, he stood right next to Alanna that Alanna could feel the hard ripple of his arm muscle on her arm. His eyes widened in worry as he stared at Alanna.

"I found this-this brochure, this paper with information about grad school. It was at the back pocket of the clothes I wore when I was taken here." Alanna lifted the brochure and showed it to Tristan. Tristan took the brochure and spent a moment looking at it.

"Grad school. That is what you want to do, isn't it?"

"Yes. I do, Tristan. That is what I want to talk to you about. I-I want to go back to my universe. To do what I have always wanted to do."

"Grad school and dogwalking."

"Yes."

"And you are worried that-that going home to your universe will influence ... us."

"Us. Yes. I mean, seriously. Are we on a relationship here? Is there an us? I am not sure, I—"

Tristan tilted his head and he looked wounded. "I do not just kiss any girl and pretend nothing happens, Alanna."

"I-I am just not sure. I guess I need solid confirmation. You know. Proper words."

Tristan took a deep breath, and his eyes looked so serene it calmed Alanna down too. "I love you, Alanna. I have always loved you, and will always do. Is that solid enough?" Alanna gasped for air, Tristan had shown her how special she was to him before, but to have the proclamation out in such solid sentence right now, that did surprise her.

Tristan grew uneasy, and stuttered,"I-I I hope you feel the same. I am not-not good with words. I do not mean to make it awkward, you know. I-I..."

"Love is such a big word, Tristan. I am scared of using it, to be honest. Though I do think you are special to me. I do like you a lot. I really do."

Tristan gazed outside for a few seconds, then turned to her and smiled,"We have time, Alanna. You and me. Us. We have time to see where we are going, to get to know each other."

Tristan lifted his hand and caressed Alanna's cheek. "I want you to be happy, to chase your dreams."

"We will live in different universes then."

"I will be faithful to you if that is what worries you. I will visit you, and I would love to see your universe too. Our beloved Pan's door will always be there for us to use."

Alanna smiled. Maybe Tristan was the one for her. Maybe, who knew? She had a failed one before, and this time, maybe she had found the one for her. Time would decide. A king from a snowy land, in a different universe, where dragons flew and sorcery happened. Apparently that was what it took for her to find her love and put together pieces of her broken heart.

"The death of Thyrra means spring would come again. Alathyr's winter will be over soon. Come visit here again when it is spring. It is beautiful," Tristan slowly took her waist and hugged it.

Tristan bowed his head slightly to let his forehead touched Alanna's, and they spent some time in silence, with their hands holding each other's back. There was not really any need for words, and it was peaceful.

"Come in the spring, Alanna. I would love to show you Alathyr. The majestic mountains and forests and lakes. The dragons' would take a dive into the lakes, and their scales glisten under the spring sunshine. You would love the scenery. Things would be a bit more settled here by then, we can spend a lot of time together."

"Visit me and my universe too, Tristan. I have so much to show you!"

"I will, Alanna. I will. I know I cannot just take the dragons with me, but Filip. He will come along. He would hate me if I go without him to visit you. That old gentleman has decided since day one that he loves you."

Alanna laughed. "I do seem to have a way with dogs. And dragons."

Tristan lifted her chin and she smiled. When he kissed her lips, she could feel the warmth that turned to a source of flame within her body. Tristan just felt right for her. She had no idea how to describe it. His strength, his gentleness, his broken heart, his wounds, his love ... all.

She knew a new part of her life had begun, here in the snowy land of Alathyr. A life that she had just discovered, a life she did not know that it existed.

Big decisions about her life had to be made in the future, she had to prepare herself for those too. To be a dragon healer was her destiny, and she had to learn to get used to that.

But here and now in this room, there were only Tristan and her. That was what mattered: Being us.

As her bare skin touched his, there was a sense of inevitability, like a massive gulf of waves that engulfed them, awakened all their senses in excitation and corporeal pleasure.

She slowly disentangled herself from Tristan's embrace, and he groaned as she pushed him gently and he sat on the edge of her bed.

"There are doors that need to be closed, Tristan. Doors to the past that have worn out its welcome, and some doors need to be opened, those for the new people, new adventure. A new beginning."

Tristan nodded, his eyes saw through her, and he agreed with her.

"Though there is one door I need to close now," she smiled, ran her fingers on Tristan's face tattoo, and walked slowly backward to her bedroom door.

She did not take her eyes off Tristan as her right hand pushed the door.

With a gentle thud, the door closed.